SPIRIT OF THE CONDOR

Anthony Masters

Chief Mono also moved forward into the moonlight. He no longer seemed like a weak little man berating his tribe, but a figure of vengeance .... He was clearly deeply shocked and enraged. Suddenly the young Daiku threw his burden to the ground in front of them. It was Rikki Moon Shadow, two darkly winking precious stones gripped in his hands.

Green Watch is an environmental pressure group founded by Seb Howard, with his two kids, Brian and Flower, and their cousin Tim. Together they battle to protect the natural world from ruthless exploitation – campaigning against the needless slaughter of innocent creatures and the thoughtless pollution of the environment. No animal is too small for Green Watch to care about and no place too remote for them to get to. Needless to say, they manage to ruffle quite a few feathers along the way . . .

SPIRIT
OF THE
CONDOR

Book Six in the Green Watch series

by
Anthony Masters
Illustrated by Pauline Hazelwood

Hippo Books
Scholastic Publications Limited
London

Scholastic Publications Ltd,
10 Earlham Street, London WC2H 9RX, UK

Scholastic Inc.,
730 Broadway, New York, NY 10003, USA

Scholastic Canada Ltd,
123 Newkirk Road, Richmond Hill,
Ontario L4C 3G5, Canada

Ashton Scholastic Pty Ltd,
P O Box 579, Gosford, New South Wales,
Australia

Ashton Scholastic Ltd,
Private Bag 1, Penrose, Auckland,
New Zealand

First published in the UK by Scholastic Publications Limited,
1991

Text copyright © Anthony Masters, 1991
Illustration copyright © Pauline Hazelwood, 1991

ISBN 0 590 76575 2

Typeset by AKM Associates (UK) Ltd, Southall, London
Printed by Cox and Wyman Ltd, Reading, Berks

10 9 8 7 6 5 4 3 2 1

pushing their boards in front of them, struck out through the waves until they were well beyond the breaking crests. Out here, on the undulating swell, Tim felt clean inside and out and his mind was so clear that it seemed rapier sharp. They sat on their boards while Rikki explained what he had done wrong last time.

"Ready to have another go?"

"Sure."

"Let's wait for the right wave, then."

"OK, but how do you know which one it is?" asked Tim, as the enormous Pacific rollers raced their way towards the great flat strip of sandy beach.

"Instinct," grinned Rikki. "That and native cunning."

Tim looked up at the bright blue sky, laced with the odd fleecy cloud. "What's that?" he said suddenly.

Rikki glanced up and said sharply, "I don't believe it!"

"What?"

"I just don't believe it."

"Believe what?" asked Tim impatiently, paddling with his hands and looking up at the slow-wheeling, extraordinary bird. It seemed a cross between a vulture and some kind of bald-headed eagle.

"It's the condor." Rikki's voice took on a note of awe. "She's our tribe's sacred bird. I've never seen her so far afield before; she usually stays around the canyon."

"She's weird."

"She's important." On Rikki's face was an expression Tim had never seen before – mysterious and shuttered. Despite the sunlight and the warm, heaving ocean, Tim suddenly felt as if Rikki had gone away somewhere.

"You make it sound as if that condor's the only one of her kind."

"She is," said Rikki quietly. "There're a few in captivity, but that's the last wild one."

"Why is she sacred?" Tim was hesitant now, as if the question might provoke a reprimand.

Suddenly the strange look passed from Rikki's eyes and he aimed a mock punch at Tim's shoulder. But his voice was still distant as he answered: "Our legend says that the condor taught the Daiku how to dance, and if the dance is correctly performed a man could become the bird he once was." Then he laughed in embarrassment. "You'll be thinking the Daiku are crazy," he said awkwardly, "but we're not. I can tell you that."

"Is the condor protected?" asked Tim, watching the bird that was now flying out of sight over the land.

"Of course, and they say they're hoping to return the captive species to the wild. But I don't know whether that's ever going to happen. Meanwhile we, the Daiku, have the last free condor in our canyon. I don't know for how much longer." He paused, looking deeply anxious. "She must be pretty old now."

"How long do they live?"

"I'm not sure. I don't think I want to know," said Rikki slowly. "Any day she could just drop out of the sky. What's more, she has only ever been known to lay an egg once a year and she hasn't got too much

4

chance of that, all on her own."

"What will the Daiku do then?"

For a moment Rikki looked shuttered again, then he smiled at Tim. "Come on, let's go for a wave."

"Haven't you ever seen the condor over the sea before?" asked Tim.

"No." Rikki's reply was abrupt and it was obvious that he didn't want to continue the conversation. "This is the one," he said and the wave took them on its crest. Tim stood up on the board and this time he didn't fall off. He lost sight of Rikki, and of everything else, while he coasted on the great wall of growling water, landing in the shallows miraculously the right way up and with his board beneath him.

"That was great!" said Rikki, suddenly appearing beside him, the water glistening on his dark skin in shining droplets. "Really good stuff." He sounded elated, but Tim noticed that before picking up his board he gazed up into the sky warily. Apart from the wheeling seagulls it was empty. The condor had gone.

An hour later, Brian, Flower and Tim were sitting on the beach with Rikki, eating a picnic. They had come to California for a much-needed holiday. It was early autumn and they had spent the Easter holidays in Africa, battling to save the lives of some gorillas – an adventure they had written up for the *Natural World Magazine*. Brian had had a bout of malaria when he got home, and this was the main reason for all three of them tacking a few extra days on to half term and using the magazine's fee to pay the airfare to Los Angeles.

Originally Flower had been determined to give the magazine fee to her parents, to help the ailing finances of the Howard family. However, Seb and Anne, back on brief leave from an environmental project at the South Pole, convinced her that the trip to California would be good for Brian. Seb had worked with the Daiku many years ago, saving Rikki's life when he was bitten by a snake as a child, and he knew that Rikki would want to repay the debt.

The sun began to set over the Pacific, the magnificent rollers turning a deep crimson as they continued to thunder up the beach.

"We saw the condor." said Tim and began to explain, but Rikki cut him short.

"She's the Daiku's sacred bird – the one and only – but it's bad luck to talk about her." His voice was strained and he peeled an orange very carefully and precisely, as if consciously forcing himself to stay calm. Brian and Flower looked at him in surprise, wondering at the sudden tension in him but not liking to say anything.

Brian and Flower were brother and sister and Tim was their cousin. His father had recently come out of prison and now had a job. He and Mum were very happy, but he knew that he had a second, supportive family in the Howards. Together with Seb and Anne, they had formed a small environmental protection group called Green Watch, and had already had several adventures. Tim didn't think anything would

6

happen in California, though – they were here for a holiday, and to make sure Brian really got better. Soon after their return home Seb and Anne would finish their project at the South Pole and Green Watch would be re-united.

"Here they come!" Flower remarked suddenly, looking up. "This is the moment I love best."

They watched as the inhabitants of the little town of Coronado began to stroll down to the beach as they often did in the evening to watch the sunset. It was a moving sight as the molten sun slid over the horizon and the waves changed from fiery red to sombre purple.

"Let's go up on the boardwalk and have a coffee," said Rikki. "Then we'll go back to the cabin."

Rikki Moon Shadow rented a little shack on the waterfront which he used as a base when he left the canyon to make some money as a surf instructor. This was Green Watch's last day on the coast for a while as he was taking them back to the reservation to meet his people. Tim was looking forward to that – to meeting real American Indians and seeing how they lived, although Rikki emphasised that the Daiku were not representative. "We have our own very special shrine and belief, although there aren't many of us left now," he had told him sadly.

Suddenly Tim was jerked abruptly back to the present as Rikki sprang to his feet, staring down the shadowed beach.

"What's the matter?" asked Flower.

"Thought I saw someone."

7

"There it goes!" Tim was on his feet too. "Right up against the skyline – don't you see the condor's silhouette?" But then he wasn't sure whether he had seen it or not and all Brian and Flower were aware of was a fleeting black shadow in the sky. Rikki, however, was still staring down the beach at the crowds who were walking slowly and contentedly back to the small town.

"I'm sure I saw a man with a gun," he said.

"Where?" asked Brian, scanning the beach.

"He was pointing it at the sky."

"I don't see —" Tim stared up and down. Then he spotted a figure hurrying up towards the road, with something tucked under his arm. Was it a gun? It was almost impossible to tell.

"He was going to kill the condor," whispered Rikki.

There was a long silence, punctuated by the muffled crashing of the surf and the slushing sound it made as it was dragged back over the smooth sand.

"He's gone," said Flower, taking his arm gently.

Rikki looked at her miserably. "Maybe he'll be back."

The boardwalk ran down the side of the harbour and the café had tables outside, overlooking the moored yachts and the winking lights of cars on the vast suspension bridge. They ordered mugs of hot chocolate and coffee and succumbed to the wonderful glow of complete physical exhaustion.

"How long will the journey be tomorrow?" asked Flower.

"Three hours in the pick-up," said Rikki. "Then we'll be in Palm Canyon."

"How many of the tribe are left?" asked Brian. They had hardly discussed the Daiku, for they had seemed to inhabit a different and mysteriously alien world from the surfing beaches of the Californian coastline. What was more, Rikki had not encouraged much conversation about them either. Tim had found it hard to picture the Indians and Flower and Brian had agreed. All they could imagine were Indians from old Western films they had seen on rainy Sunday afternoons at home – chanting and dancing round a fire or ambushing cavalry men with phoney-sounding war cries. The cinema had turned the American Indian into a stereotype, and it was very difficult to see Indians as anything other than war-painted braves.

"Not many in the canyon – about fifty," said Rikki, opening up for the first time. "There are others, but they come and go from the towns. There used to be hundreds of us, but there's nothing left to live on. Tourists, the souvenir shop, growing fruit, making craft objects – that's all we do now. It's shameful. We lost our dignity as well as our livelihood. We had cattle and we could grow wheat, but now that's all been taken away from us." He paused and then continued, as if warming to his curious audience. "We used to live in the desert in winter where the ground was still warm from sunshine and then go back to the canyon in summer where it's cool and

9

there were still streams coming down from the mountains." He paused again. "It's a wonderful place; it's home. I wouldn't ever want to leave Palm Canyon permanently. I'd fight for the Canyon; I'd die for it."

He sounded rather dramatic but they knew he meant every word. As they listened Rikki Moon Shadow had become transformed, proving that he belonged to an ancient world and that he was still very much part of its culture. "People talk about conservation, about protecting the condor," he went on, "and they're right. But no one does anything about it." He paused and added bitterly, "And no one does anything about the Daiku either. They're in need of conservation too." His voice shook slightly and Tim longed to say something that would comfort him, but he knew there was nothing he could put into words that would be of any help at all.

Then, without warning, the mood was broken. A man had suddenly appeared at their side. He was in his mid-thirties, tall and broad-shouldered with a square, clean-shaven face. There was something in his expression that was hesitant, but it was combined with an anxious aggression.

"Why, if it isn't my old buddy Rikki Moon Shadow, – the Red Indian mystic beach bum." He stood in front of their table, grinning uneasily, as if he had taken some time in making the decision to approach them.

Rikki looked wary. He made no response at all but sipped his coffee, watching him steadily.

"You baby-minding?"

"They're friends of mine," he said reluctantly.

"OK. How are you doing?" The man made a great production of shaking hands all round.

"We're fine," said Flower.

"Brits? It's good to meet some Brits again. I see Rikki's doing no introducing so I'll have to tell you my name. It's Ray Spark, and I'm in business back there on the beach, teaching surfing and yachting full-time and a bit of chandlery thrown in. I don't do it as a little hobby like Rikki here – I've got a living to earn."

As he was talking Tim could feel a change steadily creeping into Spark's voice, from hesitant patronage to menace. His smile widened unpleasantly.

"So – did you see the condor, kids?" Spark asked abruptly. "Did you see the last wild condor in all its glory?"

Tim cast a warning look at the others. For some reason he couldn't really understand, he knew he hadn't the slightest intention of saying he had seen the bird, as if by admitting a sighting he would be betraying a secret.

"No one saw the condor?" Spark's voice grew harsher.

"No," said Tim instinctively. "No one saw anything like that."

"That's a real shame. Because I got me a challenge."

"What's that?" asked Flower.

"To shoot the darn thing right out of the skies."

"Was that you on the beach with a gun?" asked Tim in horror.

"You bet it was," winked Spark.

Chapter Two

There was a long, shocked silence from Green Watch while Rikki stared ahead as if Spark didn't exist.

"Why would you want to do that?" asked Flower, outraged.

"Piece of sport."

"It's done nothing to you," she snapped, still unsure whether he was joking or not.

"That's true enough." His grin broadened. "But it's only a bird, isn't it?"

"It's said to be the last one alive out of captivity," said Tim, too angry to continue pretending he knew nothing about it.

"So?" Spark grinned.

"That's why you can't shoot it."

"You must be sick to want to do that – if you're

really serious." Flower was contemptuous. "Really sick."

"A bird's a bird." He was grinning at Rikki now. "Isn't that right, Rikki Moon Shadow?"

"Why don't you take a jump?" said Rikki with sudden vehemence.

"Now, that's not courteous."

"You touch that bird," said Rikki, looking at him for the first time, "you harm one feather of that bird and I'll kill you."

"You threatening me?" Spark was clearly pleased that Rikki had taken the bait at last.

"It's a promise."

Ray Spark came nearer. "I'll do what I like," he said. "I'm not operating alone. There are plenty of people who'd like to see that bird die. Even an Indian friend of mine thinks the condor legend's a load of superstitious rubbish."

"An Indian?" asked Flower. "A member of the Daiku?"

"That would be telling," he sneered, but Tim wondered if Spark had suddenly realised he had said too much.

"Drop off!"

"And I don't like threats or anti-social behaviour." His smile widened, knowing that Rikki's temper was rising.

Rikki slowly rose to his feet and moved away from the table. "You want to take a walk?" he asked Ray Spark.

"I prefer to stay right here."

"I don't."

"Afraid of being shown up in front of the kids?" There was a look of sardonic amusement on Spark's face and Tim knew that all this was quite deliberate and that there was nothing that any of them could do about it. Without a second's hesitation Rikki hit Ray Spark in the mouth.

Spark fell backwards against the balustrade, recovered and put his hand to his lips. Amazingly the grin never left his face. By now a small and expectant crowd had gathered.

"Well —" He sauntered towards Rikki, "that wasn't too friendly." With a darting movement he hit out with a powerful blow that reached its target, but Rikki registered no pain as Spark's fist thumped into his stomach. He hurled himself at Spark again and in seconds the two men were locked in combat, trading blow for blow. Eventually they clinched and fell to the ground, rolling, kicking, scattering tables and customers to right and left. Neither showed any sign of winning or of tiring, until they rolled back into the balustrade which cracked ominously and then broke in two, depositing the combatants in the harbour water below.

"No one goes anywhere," said the small Italian owner of the café, emerging abruptly from its dim interior and pushing Tim back into his seat. "This damage will have to be paid for, and I expect to have the money now!"

Rikki walked back down the boardwalk, soaking

wet and with blood running down his face. He looked pleased.

"You owe me – or somebody does," said the proprietor.

Rikki reached into the zipped-up pocket of his jeans, pulled out a wallet and laid some very wet dollar bills on the table.

"That's all I've got."

"And that'll just about cover it." The owner went quickly back inside, as if by staying out he was courting disaster. "You go," he said from the safety of the doorway. "All of you – go now."

"I think he's trying to tell us something," said Rikki.

"Where's that horrible man?" asked Flower.

"He swam off. I guess he knew there'd be damage to pay for."

"But why did he —" she pursued.

"Let's go." He glanced at the dispersing crowd. "They've had their entertainment. We'll go back to the cabin." He put a hand to his ribs and winced.

"You – need a doctor?" asked Brian.

"I need a whisky," replied Rikki.

"Why did he start that?" asked Flower when they were sitting in the big main room of the cabin, overlooking the beach. Rikki had washed away most of the blood from his face, but they could see it was heavily bruised.

"He's been trying to start something for ages," he muttered vaguely, staring out at the beach and the surf lashing the shoreline, milky white under the full moon.

"Yes," said Flower. "But why?"

"I reckon he wants me out of the way for a while – like on a hospital bed." Rikki looked genuinely bewildered. "He's tried to provoke me into a fight several times, but I've resisted. I should have done that just now."

"Have you done something to him then?" Brian was completely mystified. "There must be more to it than that."

"Maybe it's to do with his girlfriend."

"Who's she?"

"She's an ocean-racer – Dinah Rush. She has more style than Spark any time, but she has a reputation for being ruthless and Spark's made of marshmallow compared to her. Her family owns an island just off the coast. I gather the place is in ruins – they lost all their money in some Wall Street crash – but she makes a living racing yachts. About six months ago she'd had enough of Ray Spark; I suppose she'd found him out for the bum he is. She hung round the beach and asked me out for a meal. I was flattered, I guess. Dinah's quite something." He paused. "It was like taking out a Rottweiler. I suppose I was fascinated by her; I even took her to the canyon. But she seemed to lose interest in me after she'd met my folks and talked to the tribe." He laughed sourly. "Maybe she didn't go for the Daiku. Anyway, she went back to Ray. Guess he wants to pay me back."

Rikki paused. He managed a trace of his old grin

16

and then yawned. "We'd better get some sleep. It's going to be a long day tomorrow."

He got up stiffly as Flower said, "You sure you're going to be OK?"

"Sure. I want to get back to the canyon – to get home."

"What about the condor?" she asked.

"What about it?"

"Is Spark really going to shoot it?"

"The condor's a her."

"*Her*, then."

"No, I don't think he will. It's just a threat to wind me up."

"Why should he want to shoot the condor?" Brian persisted.

But Rikki was already pulling out some camp beds. "You guys gonna give me a hand?" he said brusquely. "I'm bushed."

"Can we sleep outside like we did last night?" asked Tim.

"No, not with that slob wandering about."

"Wandering about?" asked Flower in alarm. "Why should he do that? Does he want to finish —"

But she never completed the sentence. "It's lights out," said Rikki commandingly, "like at summer camp – and no more talking." There was a hard edge to his voice that they had never heard before.

Tim couldn't sleep. The condor, the strange remarks Rikki had made on the beach, the fight on the boardwalk had kept his brain working all night, and by four he had only managed to drift into a light, troubled sleep. He dreamt that he was surfing beside the condor, who was also on a board and who kept croaking disapprovingly as they crested the waves.

Just then a huge yacht sped towards them with Ray Spark on the prow, levelling a rifle at the condor.

"Watch out!" said Tim, grabbing the bird and clasping it to his chest as he was wiped out by a wave. The bird started pecking him as he struggled for breath and then he woke to find Flower shaking his shoulder.

"Stop biting," he muttered.

"I haven't touched you," she giggled.

"Pecking – pecking – all the time."

"What?"

"He'll be on the next wave with his sights trained on you. Keep still!"

"Wake up, Tim!" She kept pushing at his shoulder.

"What?"

"Wake up. You're dreaming!"

He surfaced to see her staring at him, trying not to laugh.

"What's the time?" Tim muttered.

"Nearly six."

"Middle of the night."

"I couldn't sleep," she said. "And I daren't wake Brian; he's meant to be getting as much rest as he can. Do you want to go out on the beach? It's a lovely morning and the sun'll be coming up soon."

"OK." He yawned and stretched . "I couldn't sleep

18

either. I kept having this weird dream about the condor."

"I gathered it must be something to do with a bird." She giggled again. "Get up quickly and don't wake Rikki or Brian. I want to go and watch the surf."

They stood side by side on the shoreline, watching the pearly grey light just touch the top of the waves as a pale, honey-coloured sun crept up over the horizon.

"Ocean's a much better word for sea, isn't it?" she said. "Sea's rather dull and ocean's - well —"

"Romantic?"

"No, more than that. Mysterious somehow. Like the condor." She paused, watching the surf, which looked silky and insubstantial in the slight early morning mist that was creeping off the sea.

"Talking of mysterious —" began Tim.

"Rikki?"

"There's something about that bird and him and Ray Spark that he's not telling us - I'm sure of it."

Flower nodded. "You're right. He's really worried about something, but he's not going to share it."

"And I don't think the fight was just about this woman, Dinah or whatever her name was," Tim said.

"There's more in it," she muttered. "But I don't understand what it is." She looked up into the pale sky and saw something dart against the rising sun. "Look —"

"It could be anything."

"Is it the condor?"

A thrill of anticipation coursed through Tim, but then the black speck seemed to fly even higher into the light orange sky and disappeared.

Rikki's battered but brightly painted pick-up truck drove into Palm Springs just before lunch. The city was an oasis at the beginning of arid desert land. There were no skyscrapers, just cool two or three-storey buildings radiating a feeling of opulence which intensified as they drove through avenues of large houses, set back in their own grounds, each with its swimming pool. The mountains loomed behind the buildings, a marked contrast to the sophistication below.

Soon they were bumping over a rough track, climbing slowly as they began to near the foothills of the mountains. Then they came out on to a ridge, driving along it until they reached two large rocks. On the right-hand one were the faded painted words:

PALM CANYON
DAIKU INDIAN LAND
U.S. GOVERNMENT RESERVATION

Rikki sounded the horn and drove into a car-park equipped with public lavatories, a souvenir shop and a rather tatty looking café.

"Yes," he said. "This is how we make our money. Come and meet my mother – she looks after the shop."

No one dared say anything as he swung his stocky,

muscular figure out of the truck. He was looking tired and aggressive, as if he were ashamed of the sad entrance to Palm Canyon but absolutely determined not to show it.

Inside, the shop was light and airy. There were no customers but a fine display of basketwork, pictures and carved figures. Behind one of the counters stood an elderly Indian woman, dressed in a T-shirt and jeans.

"My mother – her name's Haitu," he announced. "Flower, Brian and Tim – from Green Watch."

When she smiled, they were immediately drawn to her, for Haitu's weathered, deeply lined face was wreathed in genuine welcome. "I have heard much about you," she said. "Welcome to the Canyon – we shall be having a special feast tonight in your honour. Seb Howard is still remembered here. He did us a service we can never repay." She then took a sharp look at her son's bruised face. "And you – you've been fighting with the children?"

"Not with the children, Mother."

"Then, who?"

"Someone who is unworthy of discussion."

"I see." She shrugged and suddenly smiled again. "What can you do with him?" Haitu addressed Flower directly. "He is my only son – what do I do?"

Flower didn't really know what to say, although she understood what Haitu felt. For years, before her stepmother Anne came along, she had been the only woman in a house of men, and she often felt kinship with another woman, a mother. Yet she didn't want

21

to get involved, so she contented herself with a knowing shrug which seemed to satisfy Haitu.

Then she saw the birds in the glass case – long lines of carved wooden condors. In other cases there were a large number of solitary eggs, also made of wood.

"Of course," she said. "The condor's eggs."

"Egg," replied Haitu. "That's why the breed's dying out. You can see how terrible it would be if we lost our condor. She's our symbol of life and hope, and unless we can find her a mate we shall all be finished. But as she can only lay one egg a year the odds are against us. Suppose she is infertile? Or that precious egg were to be stolen? A whole year's effort could be wiped out."

Rikki looked impatient. "I'll take them up to the village," he said, as if he didn't want to hear any more negatives.

"Very well," replied his mother, looking rather offended at being interrupted so brusquely, "I'll see you later." With that she returned to her counter.

"That condor," said Brian to Tim as they left the shop. "You just can't get away from her, can you?"

At the top of a bumpy trail, between a gushing stream and huge rocks overlooking the valley, was a cluster of teepees. But there was no one around – just a couple of sniffing dogs.

Eventually an old woman emerged from one of the teepees.

"Martha —" said Rikki urgently. "Where are they all?"

"Something's happened." Her voice trembled.

"What?" Rikki snapped and Tim could see the agitation in his eyes.

"They're up at the shrine. Someone's been there, disturbing things." Her voice was hoarse and guttural, as if she didn't use it very much. "I knew there were bad signs," she added.

"Signs?" repeated Rikki, looking slightly dazed. Tim glanced at Flower and Brian, knowing that they felt as he did - as if everything was running out of control.

"The condor —" She paused. "She went away – and you know what that means."

"She was disturbed —"

The old woman shook her head mournfully. "She deserted us, but she's returned. But if anything else happens, maybe we'll lose her. And once we lose the condor the Daiku are lost as well. You know that's true, Rikki Moon Shadow. You know, don't you?"

Rikki turned away almost as if she had hit him.

Chapter Three

"We'd better go and see what's going on." Rikki strode off up the canyon, and the other three quickly followed him along the narrow, rocky path. Around them were ancient palm trees and a gushing stream; the mountains beyond standing out in stark clarity in the clear afternoon light. A great silence seemed to hang over the canyon, and even the calling of the birds appeared to be stilled.

Rikki hurried on as the path climbed higher until they came to a plateau-like clearing. In the centre, where the stream broadened, was an extraordinary structure: a giant statue in the shape of the condor towered above them to a height of about six metres. It was made of stone, and in the folds of its mighty wings were models of men and women dancing.

Stick-like and primitive, they reminded Tim of little matchstick figures. But what was most startling were the eyes, beak, head and feet of the stone condor, all of which were studded with what looked like dozens of sparkling jewels.

"What are they?" asked Tim.

"Diamonds," said Rikki irritably.

"Blimey!"

Around the statue were grouped about fifty Indians, all of them dressed in jeans, T-shirts or cotton dresses. Male, female, old, young, they stood in little huddles while their children ran about the grass, playing.

"What's happened?" asked Rikki.

"Someone's been here while Lone Wolf slept," replied a young woman.

"How do you know?" snapped Rikki angrily. "And why was the guy asleep?"

The woman took his arm and pointed to the eye of the condor. One precious stone was hanging loose.

"You mean someone tried to prise that out with Lone Wolf asleep below? Where is he?"

A stocky man with tribal marks on his cheeks came up and said softly, "He is being punished, Rikki."

"Where *is* he?"

"Up the canyon, in one of the silent houses. He will stay there for some days, contemplating his failure."

Rikki's anger seemed to lessen and he turned apologetically to Green Watch. "I'm sorry – this is Chief Mono. He is the leader of the Daiku. These are

the members of Green Watch I was telling you about
– Flower, Brian and Tim."

The chief shook them by the hand slowly and
courteously, "I have heard about your exploits."

Flower found herself the spokesperson as the boys
seemed too embarrassed to speak, but she couldn't
really think of anything to say either. "Didn't he –
why didn't he wake up if someone was hacking away
at a diamond?"

"Just the question I was going to ask," said Rikki
approvingly.

Chief Mono shrugged. "I don't think Lone Wolf
was anywhere near the shrine – more like curled up
asleep in the grass over there." He turned back to
Flower. "The shrine has been here for hundreds of
years and is guarded – has always been guarded – by
two of our tribe every night. But as our numbers have
diminished we've been forced to use only one guard
during the day."

Rikki nodded. "This is the first attack we've had in
years, isn't it?"

Chief Mono agreed. "I have to tell you that I think
the attack on the shrine was made to test our security,
which was, of course, sadly lacking."

"You think they'll try again?"

"It's possible."

"Do you think he – the thief – was disturbed?"
asked Brian, determined to make an impact on the
conversation.

"No. I think the thief simply tried to loosen the
diamond to find out how easy it was."

"We'll have to tighten security at the gates," said Rikki.

"He didn't come that way," replied Chief Mono.

"Over the rocks? That would have been a really difficult climb."

"I'm sure that's the way this person came. Man or woman, they must have been very fit."

"It's amazing," said Flower. "How much are those precious stones worth?"

"Thousands," said Rikki. "Maybe more."

"And you let them just stand here?"

"This is a sacred place," said Chief Mono. "The spirits of our ancestors come down here from their resting places."

"Where are those?" asked Tim, speaking self-consciously for the first time.

"Beyond the silent houses – in the Forest of Dreams."

"That sounds weird," Brian blurted out, and then looked as if he wished he hadn't said anything.

But Chief Mono was not in the least offended. "It is – as you say – a very weird place. Would you like to take them up there, Rikki?"

He hesitated. "I didn't think it was allowed."

"It's not – for tourists. But for the innocents —"

"I don't think we *are* innocent," said Brian gloomily.

Chief Mono's smile broadened.

"Don't miss the opportunity," said Rikki. "The Forest of Dreams is quite something."

"We shall be preparing food," said Chief Mono. "Would you like to go up there first?"

"Yes please!" said Flower, speaking for all three of them.

"One thing," put in Brian.

"Well?"

"Aren't you going to call the police?"

Rikki laughed rather cynically. "We don't have much confidence in outside forces. We like to deal with tribal matters ourselves."

Chief Mono nodded in agreement. "We find that way to be the best."

The rocky path became steeper as they walked and the foliage dustier. The stream no longer ran alongside and the heat seemed to be intensifying, despite the fact that they were travelling upwards. Tim wondered what the others were thinking; they gave nothing away, and their expressions were unreadable.

Gradually the palm trees grew denser until they were packed amongst the rocks, making a canopy above them, blotting out the sun but retaining a dry heat that gave him a headache. Then he began to notice what looked like faded rags tied to the trees and bushes.

"What are they?" asked Flower.

"Traditional robes and head-dresses – the ceremonial clothes that belonged to the dead. They're here to ward off bad spirits coming near the Forest of Dreams." Rikki suddenly looked vulnerable. "I suppose you think we're crazy."

"No," said Brian hastily.

"You'd be forgiven if you did." Rikki smiled gently. "You have to understand we've been on this continent since the dawn of time; the white man hasn't been here very long. They thought they were the civilised society and we were the savages. But the truth is that it's the other way round; we have the civilisation. It's been forced back into the reservations now, but it's still there." He looked around him. "It's here."

Rikki turned and began to walk on until they reached another small clearing. Two round wooden huts stood there. There were no windows in either of them, nor was there any sign of a door.

"Are they punishment cells?" asked Tim.

Rikki paused and grinned, but the grin was a shadow of his old one. He was a different person from the one he had been on the Pacific beach. Here, in his own land, he should have been just as relaxed – if not more so. But instead, forcibly reminded of so many problems, he was becoming tense and guarded. "No, that's not the way we run our society. If somebody's done something wrong they go away and think about it, maybe a couple of days in one of the silent houses. You go in underneath – there's a dug-out entrance – and you bring enough food and drink to last for the duration. Then, when you've thought it all through, you come and talk about it with the elders."

Tim nodded; it sounded quite a good system, although he wondered how well it worked. But he could see that Rikki still looked troubled.

"What's up?" he asked. "You look really worried."

"Isn't there enough to be worried about?" said

Rikki. "The desecration of the shrine and —"

"No," said Flower. "There's more, isn't there?"

"What is it?" asked Brian sharply.

"Move up a bit, away from the silent houses," Rikki said.

They did as he told them and gathered a little further up the rise.

"This tribe's dying," Rikki said. "Most of us have left the reservation for the towns, and what's left? Old people, a few young with a few kids. And they'll be gone soon. Our way of life is vital, but most of us have to live and work outside, like I do at Coronado. All we've got is Palm Canyon – our tribal lands have been stolen by the government."

"But that was a long time ago," said Brian.

"Sure, but now the end's coming, I'm certain of it, and it's not as if it's happening naturally."

"What do you mean?" asked Tim.

Rikki's face was strained. "The tribe's been so weakened that if anyone wanted to destroy it, it would be easy. Just imagine the scenario: you shoot the condor, you rob the shrine. The Daiku would fold up – just like that."

"Where would they go?"

"They'd drift away; even Chief Mono would find somewhere else in the end."

"If it's so fragile, would it last anyway?"

"Given a chance. I've got a lawyer working for us, and he reckons there's a possibility of suing the U.S. government for the return of our lands – or some of them. If we could do that, we could have cattle again, or grow crops. Maybe oranges."

"In the desert?" asked Tim.

"Not all our lands were in the desert; some stretched towards the coast where it's fertile. Even if we had *something* we could make a living and maybe attract other members of the tribe back."

"Are you saying somebody's sabotaging what's left?" asked Tim.

"I don't know," he said uneasily.

"Suppose they are?" said Brian.

"If they are, they'd stand to gain a lot."

"The shrine?"

"If we grew careless, they could take all the stones."

"You seem to be asking for it," said Brian, "having that statue – all those precious stones – just standing around in the open like that."

"It's holy ground," said Rikki quietly, and Tim realised that he really disliked any hint of criticism. "Where the condors first nested. And the condors contain the spirits of our ancestors."

"Who could have attacked the shrine?" asked Brian. "Do you have any idea?"

"No, but Lone Wolf might help us," said Rikki suspiciously. "He's young – in his twenties – and he's recently returned from L.A. He's been away since he was a teenager. Of course, many of the others have been in the city, but there's something about Lone Wolf that I don't trust." Rikki paused.

"You mean – he could be mixed up in this?" asked Flower.

"I don't know. I could be imagining things."

"Could anyone sell those precious stones?"

"Maybe. There wouldn't be much of a hue and cry over an Indian treasure," Rikki added sadly.

"And no one's prepared to move the shrine to a place of safety?" asked Brian impatiently.

Rikki shook his head. "It must be here," he said. "Nowhere else." He sounded adamant.

"Is the condor really at risk?" Tim was beginning to wonder what they had all let themselves in for by coming to Palm Canyon. "It's difficult to know where to start."

"We can start with Lone Wolf," said Rikki grimly. "I need to find out exactly what happened."

"How do we do that?" Flower was mystified. If Lone Wolf was involved with the theft he wasn't likely to admit anything.

"I don't know," said Rikki, some of his confidence draining away. "I've been trying to think —"

"Let *us* help," said Brian suddenly.

"You're meant to be —"

"Yes, I know. Taking it easy. But I've done that, and I'm fine." He turned to the others. "Doesn't all this look like another Green Watch project?"

The other two nodded rather doubtfully while Rikki gave them a slow, hesitant smile. "I could use some help," he admitted. "I really could. Maybe it's because I've been away to college, but I'm finding the Daiku increasingly dependent on me – and it's lonely, really lonely."

32

As they walked on, the palm trees thinned out, those that remained looking almost dead, with black leaves and withered trunks. The bushes, however, festooned with the ceremonial clothing, grew closer and higher until they almost resembled a tunnel overhanging a well-worn path that led into a small forest. The trees here were redwoods, standing like sentinels amongst wide clearings, and it was hard to see the sky above, for the higher branches shut out most of the light. On the ground were dozens of long black poles, each about six metres high and surmounted by a carved wooden condor's head. The poles were clad in head-dresses made from highly coloured dyed feathers, and each bore a name – Running Deer, Flying Horse, Snake Man, Bone Lord, Little Fox, Anna of the Sunlight, Jon Sunset and many others. There was complete silence in the Forest of Dreams, and there seemed to be no animal – or even insect – life at all.

When Tim looked at the ground, all he could see was hard, impacted soil on which nothing grew, but there was a curiously sweet smell which reminded him of some kind of incense mixed with herbs. Beside each pole stood a long, thin container which held a burning candle. There must have been hundreds of them.

"Who replaces them and lights them again?" asked Flower wonderingly.

"The dream-keeper," said Rikki. "He's here all the time, looking after the place. He lives over there."

One of the trees with the largest trunk had a hole cut in the base. They could see a cave-like interior with rugs on the floor and what looked like flags hanging down each side, again illuminated by candles which were grouped on a kind of altar in the centre. When they drew near, they could see that the image of the condor, huge yet almost wraith-like, had been stitched into the cloth. Then Tim saw what at first he thought was a child, huddled on a prayer mat under one of the banners. The figure clambered to its feet to reveal itself as a very old man with wizened limbs, wearing a long dark shawl. His head was fleshless, like a skull, and his nugget eyes were huge and penetrating. He looks like a Martian, thought Tim – hardly human at all.

"This is the keeper," said Rikki, and the old man smiled, revealing a toothless mouth.

"Do you have – another name?" asked Flower awkwardly.

The keeper shook his head. "If I had they've all forgotten it."

Tim could see box after box of candles piled high against the inside of the trunk. Where did he sleep? On the prayer mat? And did he ever eat?

"You have heard about the shrine," said Rikki.

"The first time." The old man closed his eyes as if the news had been too much for him to bear. "The first in my lifetime. Evil days."

"We've redoubled the guard."

"There are not many of us left," the old man muttered.

"There *will* be more," said Rikki. "I promise there'll be more."

For the first time the old man looked at Flower, Tim and Brian directly. "Children," he muttered, and shook his head again as if they were an added burden.

"They're more then just kids." Rikki's voice was warm and Tim felt a glow spreading inside him.

The keeper mumbled something they couldn't hear and then said more clearly, "Rikki Moon Shadow – he is our hope. He is the only one who can bring us a future."

"That's too much of a responsibility," said Rikki haltingly. The dream-keeper was silent while everyone stared at him expectantly.

"There is bad will here," he said eventually.

There was another long pause, then Rikki prompted gently, "What do you mean, keeper?"

"It is here in our midst. We can be destroyed from within."

"What do you know?" asked Rikki.

"I know nothing."

"Then —"

"I feel. I can feel it through the dead."

"What do you feel?"

"Treachery." He turned and vanished into the candlelit shrine.

Tim thought of Lone Wolf sitting in the silent house. What was he thinking or planning to do? Or was he completely innocent after all? Suddenly he felt afraid. He had been in dangerous situations before, but this was frightening because it was unpredictable. He wasn't in the normal world any longer; he was in a world in which old magic and superstition had a lot do with survival. Looking at Rikki's determined features, he knew something else that disturbed him very much. As the keeper had said, the survival of the Daiku might well depend on what Rikki did and how he did it – whether he could really get back the tribal lands or at least some of them. In the short term, if the keeper was right and if the attack was from within as well as without, Rikki's own survival depended on how much help he got. There was no doubt that the odds could overwhelm him and Green Watch were in the thick of it. The point was, could they handle it?

Chapter Four

The shot rang out somewhere down below them and Rikki froze, raising a finger to his lips before anyone could speak. A scattering of birds soared upwards and a long silence followed. Then, with horrible clarity, a second shot rang out. This time the silence that followed seemed even more impenetrable.

Rikki was listening. Again putting his finger to his lips he whispered: "Stay here – stay here till I call. Don't move."

He was off now, running as lightly and softly as a cat, and in his eyes there blazed a deep, hard anger.

They stayed together, straining their ears, trying to remain as motionless as possible. Then Tim was conscious of Flower watching something to the right of them, where the bare rock of the mountain began. Lower down they could hear the rushing of the stream. Perhaps it came out from underground, he thought irrelevantly. Suddenly he saw a shadow against the face of the rock, just out of the sunlight that penetrated the fringe of palm trees in long shafts. The shadow sharpened. It was Ray Spark and he was climbing over the rock with amazing agility.

"What's he doing here?" whispered Flower. "We can't let him go."

"We'd be fools to follow him," said Brian. "It's steep up there. Rikki'll want to deal with him if he's got anything to do with this."

"Maybe he hasn't seen him," said Flower.

"I don't know —" Tim sounded hesitant, for he was the least proficient climber of them all and had always had a fear of heights. "Perhaps we should wait for Rikki."

"I'll go," she said firmly.

"No —" Brian was furious. "He told us to wait here."

"He doesn't know what's happening," she replied.

"Flower —" began Tim.

But she was too impatient for them. "I'm going." And she began to run towards the rock.

"We can't let her go alone," snapped Brian. "That's even more dangerous."

"Come on then," Tim said, ashamed of his fears, and they began to run, following her over the rough, uneven ground. Eventually they caught up with her and all three began to climb up and away from the shadows of Palm Canyon and out on to the bare, sun-baked mountainside.

Suppose Spark's shot the condor? was the thought uppermost in Tim's mind as he followed the others over the rock. At first the climb wasn't difficult – more of a sloping ascent that anything else. But after a few minutes the ground rose steeply and he realised, with creeping unease, that they were beginning to ascend a promontory that was sheer on either side and that the terrain was narrowing. For the first few minutes he didn't look down, then he did and realised what a precarious position he was in. He wished the others were with him, but they were far ahead now, moving swiftly, although there was no sign of Ray Spark.

Somehow Tim stumbled on, realising that he was now climbing a narrow ledge, praying that his fear would not force him to look down again. For a while it didn't, as he kept his eyes on Flower and Brian climbing the side of the mountain, gaining height all the time, gradually getting smaller as they did so. He struggled to catch up, but they seemed like mountain goats. Unbelievably, the ledge narrowed still further until he realised he was crossing a saddle between two crests. His throat was dry and the sun was beginning to burn the back of his neck. Unable to prevent himself any longer, Tim looked down. Below him was a small gully that sloped towards a sheer drop. Crouched in the gully was Ray Spark.

Tim paused, meeting Spark's eyes, quite unable to decide what to do next. He swayed slightly and a sudden feeling of total disorientation seized him. He could feel his legs shaking, wobbly and frail, depriving him of stability. Still he gazed straight into Spark's eyes and saw no hostility; there was even a hint of concern. Tim began to sway and Spark said gently, "OK, son – just relax."

Still Tim swayed.

"I said, relax."

The swaying continued, and although he tried to balance himself he seemed to have no control whatsoever over his limbs. The ground, many metres below, seemed to come up at him and then recede. One moment he could see palm trees close up; the next they were tiny specks, like a child's toys, neatly arranged to form a game.

"Stay there, son. I'm coming up."

There was a loud buzzing in Tim's ears now.

"What's your name?" asked Spark gently.

"Tim."

"OK, Tim. Why don't you get down on your hands and knees?"

"I can't move."

Spark began to climb up towards him, with deft, swift movements. "You've no reason to be afraid of me." His voice was gently commanding. "Absolutely no reason at all. Try to get down on your hands and knees."

"I'm going to fall."

"No, you're not."

40

"I *am*."

"Hands and knees."

"I *can't*."

"Now!" His voice was stern but he was still talking softly. "Come on, Tim. Do what I tell you."

"I'm falling."

"Hands and knees."

"No."

"Now!"

Tim fell like a stone towards the edge of the gully.

He rolled over and over, down the sloping ground. Ray Spark made a grab for him and missed. The rolling continued and Tim hadn't the faintest idea of where he was or what he was doing. Blind panic seemed to have swallowed him as he tumbled over and over, his eyes wide open but seeing nothing except the tiny palm trees and the rushing, propelling air around him. Then, in seconds, he was over the edge of the gully and plunging through the air to the canyon below.

A gigantic tremor shook Tim's body and he was jerked back and then forward – and back again. At some point during his rapid descent he must have shut his eyes, or lost consciousness for a fraction of a second. When he opened his eyes again, he was lying on a narrow strip of flat projecting rock, and his T-shirt, now ripped to shreds, was caught up in the dead branches of some kind of spiky bush. He could feel blood running down his arm. Below him, the palm trees, now looking much bigger, drew him on downwards.

"Hold on."

Tim said nothing.

"Hold on – I'm coming." The voice didn't bear a trace of panic and was as quiet and gentle and unhurried as it had been before. Tim stared down at the ground; the tops of the trees began to come towards him, and then recede again. His arms, which were hugging the slender outcrop of rock, seemed to weigh a ton.

"I'm going to fall," he said in what he imagined was a whisper.

But Spark seemed to hear him. "No, you're not."

"I can't hold on."

"If you don't, I'll give you the biggest thrashing of your life."

The crazy illogicality of Spark's remark didn't occur to Tim, and it held him.

"Please," he moaned.

"You stay where you are." Spark's voice was sharp and resolute. "If you don't, it'll be the worse for you."

Something was flying beside him, below him and above him. From somewhere a long way away, Tim heard Spark cursing.

"The condor," he said. "Is that the condor?"

"Yes, it is."

"It's flying beside me."

"Below you, actually." Spark's voice was grim.

"Will it help me?"

"Sure it will – if you stay still."

"I'm slipping."

"No. The condor'll see you OK." There was total assurance in Spark's voice.

"Going now."

"Wait for the condor, son."

"No."

"Here it comes."

There was a fluttering above him and he saw the bird soar upwards, higher and higher into the sky. But it wasn't a condor – it was just some sort of hawk.

"It isn't the —"

"No." He felt an arm grip his waist. "No, it's not the condor but you thought it was." Spark gave a laugh. "Stay still – I'm going to rip what's left of this shirt off you and then I'm taking you back up. You don't do anything, son. Do you understand?"

"Yes."

"Really nasty dose of vertigo. So you can't take heights?"

"No."

"So keep still. Shut your eyes."

"But —"

"I said, shut your eyes. If you don't, I'll shut them for you. Get it?"

"Yeah." Tim shut his eyes as Spark ripped off his T-shirt. Then he felt himself being lifted under one strong arm as Spark climbed back into the gully again.

"Don't move."

"OK."

"Now, open your eyes."

Slowly he did as he was told. All Tim could see was Ray Spark's rugged face.

"That's better."

"Thanks."

"How do you feel?"

"Sick."

"Well, don't throw up all over me." He grinned and there was a warm light in his eyes that Tim had not seen yesterday evening. "Just relax and stay where you are. I'm holding you. When you feel better, I'm going to take you down."

"I'm sorry."

"Why?"

"It was awful. Things kept swaying about."

"Vertigo. It affects the balance."

"You saved my life," said Tim in muzzy surprise. "No one's ever saved my life before."

He laughed. "I guess they haven't needed to."

"Where are the others?"

"Looking for me – a good long way away, I hope."

"Someone's trying to kill the condor." Tim closed his eyes.

"Maybe."

"Was it you?"

"No way."

"Then who was it?"

"I've no idea."

"But what *are* you doing here?"

"I'm not after the wretched bird." Again there was conviction in Spark's voice.

"Did you try to take that diamond out of the shrine?"

"No."

"Then who?"

"You can guess that."

"Lone Wolf?"

"That's the guy."

"So why are you here?" Tim didn't feel suspicious, merely curious.

"I was looking for Rikki Moon Shadow."

"Why?"

"Guess I wanted to finish the fight."

"He took your girlfriend?" asked Tim.

"For a while, until she saw sense."

"If you've got her back, why do you want to fight him?"

"He really got to me. He's so arrogant. But now I don't want the hassle – I think it must have something to do with helping you."

"Rescuing me."

"Whatever."

"Do you mean that?"

"Yes. I'll leave him alone now." But there was a glibness in his voice that made Tim, even in his still shocked condition, vaguely uneasy.

"You came a long way to fight him."

"Anger's a pretty strong motive for making a journey."

"How do you know about Lone Wolf?"

45

"That's easy. I knew him in L.A. as Mike Weston – small-time petty crook. He came back here a few months ago and convinced the tribe that he wanted to join them again. All he's after is the shrine."

"And the condor?"

"No, just the precious stones. He wanted me to join him at one point, but I've got a business to run. Don't want that kind of problem. OK, so the shrine's worth a fortune, but it doesn't interest me." He stood up, pulling Tim to his feet. "How do you feel?"

"Shaky."

"OK. I'm going to take you back to the lower rocks. You stay there and wait for your friends to come back – or Rikki to show up. You promise you'll do that?"

"I promise."

"And not go wandering off?"

"No way."

"Right. I'll take you down and then I'll disappear. If Rikki finds me here there could be a nasty misunderstanding."

"Yeah."

"Give me your arm then, and I'll keep you steady."

Slowly Ray Spark guided Tim back on to the promontory and within minutes they had returned to the lower rocks.

"Here OK?"

"Fine," said Tim.

"I'm going." He began to climb up again.

"Wait!"

"Well?"

"Thanks – thanks for what you did."

"It's all right, son. We probably won't see each other again. So take care."

Tim waved, and Spark began to bound over the rocks with incredible speed.

Tim sat on the rocks and stared up at the mountains and, in particular the incredible ascent he had failed to make. He didn't feel ashamed, just so glad to be alive that he hugged himself in delight. He would always be in Ray Spark's debt now. Looking at his watch he saw that it was four o'clock and he was starving. Yet nothing could spoil his elation and hunger only sharpened his zest for life. He looked down at Palm Canyon, somnolent in the afternoon heat, and thought how his life had so suddenly narrowed down to this tiny place which was a complete world of its own. He had only been here for a few hours and yet with the shrine, the tribe, the silent houses, the Forest of Dreams and its keeper and then the terrifying narrow escape he had had, it was as if he had lived a lifetime here.

He heard a tiny sound behind him and looked round. The condor was standing a few metres away from him, staring at him through bulbous eyes.

The bird made a curious clicking sound as Tim stared back, hardly daring to breathe. She was the most extraordinary looking creature he had ever seen – her body was black, her feet white, and her head and neck pink. Somehow she seemed very old and her eyes were wise and reflective. It was only an impression, and Tim was not sure whether he was making it up or not, yet there was something in those black eyes that were holding his own – something that was deep and profound and affected him inside. The eyes made him think of eternity and the timelessness of the canyon and the Indian way of life. They also made him think of himself, rolling into death and coming out the other side, saved by a miracle as well as Ray Spark. Did this bird of wonder have something to do with it? Had the condor also saved his life in some magical way? Of course it was crazy to think this way, and yet maybe the condor really was a source of life and the Indians were right to think that if the bird died they would die too.

Tim kept looking into the condor's eyes and began to feel he was being hypnotised slowly. What did he see in those dark pupils? Just his own reflection or the source of life itself?

Chapter Five

As soon as she heard the scrambling sound, the condor took off, fluttering up into the brilliant blue of the scorching sky. Tim saw Rikki Moon Shadow's head appearing. He looked cross and tired.

"Where on earth have you been?" he asked abruptly.

Tim explained, his elation making his story sound almost incredible. When he had finished, Rikki simply said, "And you were fool enough to believe him?"

"What?" Tim gasped.

"That man's here to rob the Daiku, and very likely Lone Wolf's in league with him."

"No – he said he'd come to settle a score with you."

"Rubbish!"

"Rikki —"

"I said, rubbish. He's completely hoodwinked you."

"He saved my life!" Tim yelled angrily.

'You shouldn't have been up there in the first place."

"We were trying to help you."

"Yeah – I told you to stay where you were." He was completely adamant but Tim was very angry.

"You're meant to be looking after us," he said childishly, but it was the only thing he could think of saying. "Instead of that I nearly died. And Ray saved me."

"So it's Ray now, is it?" snapped Rikki.

"I wouldn't be here if he hadn't —"

"How naïve can you get?"

"You make me sick!" bawled Tim.

They stood confronting each other, hot and angry tears pricking at the back of Tim's eyes.

"OK," said Rikki at length.

"And we haven't even had anything to eat," said Tim bitterly. "So I don't think much of Daiku hospitality. In fact I think it stinks!" He said the last few words so vehemently that Rikki burst out laughing.

"Get you!" he said. The mockery was too much for Tim and he hurled himself furiously at Rikki, punching and kicking at him so hard tht Rikki fell back a couple of paces and held him with one hand. Then he said, "Hey, I'm sorry." But Tim continued to attack him. "Please – look – I'm sorry." Slowly Tim subsided. "I'm really sorry."

"OK."

"I don't want to be bad friends." Rikki grabbed Tim's shoulders and hugged him. "Look, I mean it. I got myself in a mess. I guess I'm so worried about the Daiku that – and it *is* my fault that you nearly fell. Will you forgive me?" Rikki looked so genuinely penitent that Tim's anger faded.

"I'm sorry too," he said.

"Where are the others?"

"They're good at climbing," Tim said. "They'll have gone a long way now."

"And they're coming back," said Rikki. "Look, they're up there on the ridge."

Tim could just make out the distant specks running along the treacherous mountain path. How he envied them, able to run so fast in such a vulnerable position.

"So," said Rikki, "Flower's afraid of water – and you're not."

"Yeah."

"And Brian must have some kind of phobia."

"He hates spiders."

"Well, there you are," Rikki concluded.

But Tim didn't think anyone else's fears mattered; he just wished he could conquer his own.

"Rikki?"

"Yes."

"Can you climb?"

"A bit."

"Would you teach me?"

"Sure I will. But you'll never totally lose your fear of heights; it's part of your make-up."

"But can I live with it?"

"Yes. I do."

Tim looked at him in amazement. "You mean – you're afraid too?"

"Always have been. We'll try to sort something out together."

"Thanks. By the way, the condor's back." He was surprised that his anger had been so strong that he had quite forgotten this vital information. "She was sitting next to me, kind of staring at me."

"I suppose she wasn't laying an egg at the time?" asked Rikki sardonically.

There was a long silence while they both watched Flower and Brian jogging nearer.

"Where were you?" asked Tim, suddenly remembering that Rikki had not mentioned the shot they had heard. "Did you discover who fired that shot?"

"I couldn't see anyone with a gun but I stopped by the silent houses and Lone Wolf was missing. I started to search for him but it was no good. I checked everywhere but there was no sign of him. Maybe he's taken off – back to the city."

"Do you think he's linked with Spark?"

"I'm sure of it; we haven't seen the last of him."

"Are you *sure* that Spark is a villain?"

"Yes. It was great he rescued you. I suppose even the most evil person's capable of doing some good. But it's no use you having faith in him, Tim. I'm sure you'll end up horribly disillusioned."

But Tim couldn't agree, although he knew there

was no point in arguing. "We'll have to see," he said guardedly.

Flower and Brian were much more impressed than Rikki at the story of Ray Spark's intervention on the rocks. Flower in particular seemed very upset. Back at the canyon, after a welcome meal, they sat and relaxed under the palm trees. As soon as Rikki went to talk to Chief Mono, Flower said, "I don't know that we should go on being mixed up in all this. Maybe we could persuade Rikki to run us back to the beach. We could look after ourselves there."

It was so unlike Flower to back off that both boys were very startled.

"You mean drop it all?" asked Brian.

"We can't," said Tim. "We just can't. Not now."

"But you nearly got killed."

"So?"

"It's getting too dangerous."

"What's really the matter, Flower?" asked Brian persuasively.

She looked around her. Most of the tribe were sitting on the scrubby grass, eating, with the teepees as a timeless backdrop. They were friendly yet withdrawn, and although Rikki had returned to his old casual self there was still a difference in him, as if one part of him were alien and the rest going through the motions of sharing experiences with them. Haltingly she tried to put her feelings into words. "We don't belong here – can't belong. The Daiku may be dying out, may be threatened, but they're completely self-contained. It's as if they're living in a different time from us and we don't exist for them. It's so weird. Look at them now – it's as if they don't see us."

It was true. The Daiku were huddled in small groups, talking, eating, laughing – an entity yet totally apart.

"I'm sorry," Flower went on. "Don't think I'm underestimating what happened. It's just that I've got a very bad feeling about what's going on here. There's an atmosphere of horrible expectancy."

"Yes." Brian was immediately with her. "I can see that. Look, Flower, if you're really worried we *can* go back to the beach."

"No." She shook her head with sudden resolution. "I was wrong. We've got to see it through. Rikki has such faith in us we can't let him down. And besides, there's something else."

"What's that?" asked Tim.

"Look at them. Over three-quarters of the Daiku are old; there're just a few young families and they've got tiny children. They're helpless somehow, just sitting around, waiting for something to happen, and there's nothing they can do to stop it." She sounded very sure. "There's only Rikki and us. So however outside it all we feel, we've *got* to stay and face whatever's going to happen. I'm sorry, I was being weak."

"Do you know," said Tim, "I've got this very

54

strong feeling that whatever *is* going to happen, is going to happen very quickly. Haven't you?"

Brian nodded. "I think it's what everybody's thinking," he said.

Chapter Six

For the rest of the evening, Brian, Flower and Tim were hard pushed to find something to do, and ended up playing cards. Rikki had disappeared completely, and when his mother asked them where he was they said they didn't know, although all three were sure he was searching for Lone Wolf.

The sun went down, leaving Palm Canyon cooler and rather eerie. Its former stillness gone, the palm fronds rustled in a quickening evening breeze, and the Daiku went into their teepees without asking any of the trio whether they wanted company or not. Morosely they played on, each feeling lonely and unwanted. Waves of homesickness for his parents began to surge through Tim, and when he looked at Brian and Flower he was certain that they were feeling the same. It was worse for them because Seb and Anne were still at the South Pole and not due back for at least a month.

Suddenly Tim was conscious that a figure had come out of one of the teepees and was walking towards them in the twilight. As it came nearer he realised that it was Chief Mono.

"Has Rikki returned?" he asked.

"No," said Flower rather mournfully.

"He should be back by now." The Chief looked fearfully up the canyon as the night wind rattled at the palms. "The storm wind is beginning."

"What's that?" asked Brian.

"Soon there will be an electric storm; it's always preceded by this wind, hot and dry from the desert."

Sure enough the next gust was warm and they could almost smell the desert sand.

"He's looking for Lone Wolf," said Tim uneasily. "But he's been gone for hours."

"Yes, I'm worried about him."

"Couldn't he have taken some other members of the tribe with him?" asked Flower accusingly. "He seems to be the only person round here who *does* anything."

The Chief nodded. "You will have noticed how apathetic the people are here."

"But why? Don't they want to fight?" asked Brian.

"They have – for many years. But now most of them are old, and the younger ones are leaving. It is only Rikki who really believes in a future for us."

"The wind's getting up," said Tim.

There was a low growl of thunder in the west and black clouds scudded over the canyon.

"What could have happened to him?" asked Flower rather wildly. Tim knew exactly how she felt; with Rikki gone, their last link with a familiar adult had disappeared.

More thunder growled and its presence seemed to make Chief Mono as irresolute as the rest of his tribe.

"Can't we go and look for him or something?" demanded Flower. "Anything would be better than sitting here and doing nothing."

"He could be anywhere," muttered the Chief.

"But we could try," said Brian.

"No, it is better to —" He never finished the sentence, for a fluttering and beating of wings came from overhead and the condor flew into view. But her flight was ragged, and even in the semi-darkness they could see that one of her wings was beating awkwardly.

"Something's wrong," said Tim fearfully.

The bird landed and settled on a patch of ground a few metres away, her eyes fastened on them.

"She's hurt," said Flower.

"I'll look." Chief Mono went towards the condor and gently reached out. He withdrew his hand instantly and Tim could see blood running down between his fingers. "She attacked me," the Chief muttered.

"Only because she's hurt."

"No."

"What else?" gasped Flower. "She's frightened."

"It is written."

"What's written?" snapped Tim. He had had enough of superstition. Surely that was what made the Daiku so inert – so unwilling to take the initiative.

"If the condor takes a Daiku's blood, then the bird is inhabited by an enemy." The old man's voice trembled.

"Rubbish!" said Flower. "You can't *believe* that."

He turned to her angrily. "Who are you to tell me?"

"I'm sorry, but —"

"You know nothing." His voice was suddenly very savage and contemptuous. "You come here, deriding our traditions —"

"We didn't," protested Brian.

"You live in the material world," snapped Chief Mono. "We live in the spiritual. We don't want to understand your world, and you'll never understand ours." He turned back to the condor. "She's drawn blood. She's possessed."

"Who by?" asked Tim.

"Bad spirit."

"Can you identify the spirit?" asked Flower, trying to win back the old man's confidence.

"It's the spirit of Lone Wolf."

"*What*?"

"Rikki must have killed him. He's now in the condor."

Tim had never heard such nonsense. Or had he? The material, the spiritual? Maybe he didn't understand after all. The old man was terrified and he kept looking from his bleeding fingers to the condor and

59

back again. Meanwhile, the bird shifted a little, her eyes steadily fixed on them.

Flower advanced on her and the condor backed away a few centimetres. "Look at her wing," said Flower. "It's been damaged in some way. Maybe she's been shot." She paused. "Don't you remember?" She turned back to Tim and Brian. "Don't you remember what Ray Spark said just before he had that fight with Rikki —" Her voice petered out. "He said he was working with an Indian."

Yes, thought Tim. But was the Indian Lone Wolf? Or could it be someone else.

But Chief Mono wasn't listening.

"She's been shot," repeated Tim. "Don't you understand? The condor's been shot by someone. That's all – that's why she pecked you."

He still wasn't listening but was looking towards the teepees.

Brian tried one last stand. "You've got to realise – there's a perfectly natural explanation why the condor hurt you. She's in pain; we've got to help her!"

"She must die," said Chief Mono.

"*What?*"

"It's time for her to die."

"She's the last one," Tim insisted. "The very last condor. You can't kill her."

"The book says that when the condor draws blood from the Chief of the Daiku, then the condor has to die. Do you know why?"

"Yes," said Flower impatiently. "You think she's

full of evil spirits. What book are you talking about? And where is it written?"

Chief Mono stared at her sadly and Brian and Tim wondered why she was being so aggressive.

"You don't understand the ways," he said again.

"No," Flower replied. "I don't. But in this instance I don't believe your own people would understand either. You can't tell me they'd believe you. Why are you doing this?"

But Chief Mono had already turned his back on her and was making a strange calling sound – a kind of high-pitched keening which brought the Daiku out from their teepees.

Flower watched as the chief began to speak to his people in their own language, with frequent gesticulations towards the condor. The Daiku looked as bewildered as Green Watch had been a few minutes previously. Then she turned urgently to Brian and Tim.

"There's something going on."

"There certainly is," replied Brian. "But what is it?"

"I think I know," she said slowly. "I could be wrong but I've got this really strange feeling about him. It was the way Chief Mono looked at me – at first I didn't understand."

"Come *on*," said Tim impatiently. "What are you talking about?"

"He was lying," she replied.

"This is crazy," said Brian. "How on earth could you know?"

"It's just a hunch but I'm sure I'm right."

"Well, he's telling them all. Are they going to accept it?"

"I don't think he *is* saying that," said Flower. "I think he's telling them something completely different. Watch their faces."

It was certainly odd; the Daiku were looking at the condor in great sadness as if they were losing something. There was no anger – no indication that they'd been asked to kill the bird.

"Tim, don't let him see you – ask someone on the fringe of the crowd what he's saying. Try that man over there – the one that's standing on his own in the trees."

"I'll give it a go." Tim hurried away, dodging behind some bushes until he was near the Indian. "Excuse me."

But the man stared straight ahead. Did he understand? He must do; they all spoke English.

"Excuse me."

"Chief Mono is speaking."

"What's he saying?" asked Tim innocently. "We don't understand a word of all this."

"He's saying the condor is deserting us, that it's about to fly away like it did last time, but this time for good."

"How does he know?" Tim hissed.

"Look."

The condor rose and fluttered unsteadily to the top

of the palm trees. Then she disappeared.

"She'll be back," said Tim.

"No," replied the Indian.

"But —"

"We always knew she would desert us when the shrine was attacked."

A ripple of despair shivered through the ranks of the Daiku and Tim could see the misery on their faces.

"It's not true," said Tim. "It's just not true." He raced back to Flower and Brian. "He's telling them the condor's going for good, because the shrine was attacked. What's he doing, telling us one thing and the Daiku another?"

"I knew he was lying," said Flower.

Chapter Seven

"I've got an awful feeling," said Tim. "As if something's happening somewhere else."

Thunder was growling in the distance and the canyon felt hot and sultry, lifeless in the eye of the storm.

"The shrine," said Flower. "Shouldn't we go up there and see?"

If only it would rain, Tim thought – really lash down with rain and make the Daiku come alive again. But it didn't, and the storm sounded as if it were playing itself out somewhere many kilometres away.

"Hurry up," said Flower in flurry of sudden agitation. "I think something's happening up there."

They moved away from the teepees, leaving behind the silent despair of the Daiku and the drone of Chief

Mono. Once they were out of sight, they began to run as fast as they could up the canyon. As they stumbled along, tired and apprehensive, Tim felt an extraordinary emptiness, as if the soul of Palm Canyon had been spirited away and the very heart of this sacred place had disappeared.

Moonlight shone on a scene of desolation and the faraway thunder seemed like a funeral dirge played out in the sky.

"No," whispered Flower. "No!"

The great statue of the condor was leaning over at an angle and they could see that it had partly come away from its base. Ropes hung from the stone bird's neck and it looked as if an attempt had been made to pull the statue over. But this was not all – every single precious stone had been hacked away from the condor's body. It stood there, denuded, disgraced, alone, robbed of its treasure.

"We should have known," muttered Brian. "Where are the guards? There's no one here at all."

"Where's Rikki?" Flower stared round hopelessly. "A few jewels," she went on, voicing all their thoughts. "It shouldn't be the end of everything."

"It's what they stand for." Brian was impatient. "They mean everything to them – like the condor. Now all their precious stones are gone, and their sacred bird's got something wrong with its wing, they're almost finished – probably *are* finished."

Flower's voice shook with emotion. "Lone Wolf,

Ray Spark, Chief Mono – how many more are mixed up in this?"

"You don't *really* know Mono's involved," said Tim doubtfully.

"Every scrap of inituition I've got tells me he is," she replied fiercely. "He deliberately kept the Daiku down by the teepees while all this was going on. Isn't it obvious?"

Tim and Brian nodded; it did look very suspicious. They stared up again at the condor – no longer a majestic glittering life-force but a crazily tilting lump of stone. Then they heard a sound: it was a gentle, slithering shuffling – impossible to identify.

The dream-keeper emerged into the clearing. His wafer-thin body was rigid with shock and tears were pouring down his face. He stared at the broken condor and then knelt down shakily in front of the statue, muttering to himself as he did so. They watched him in distress until he dragged himself to his feet and turned to them.

"You must begin," he said obscurely, "begin now."

"What do you mean?" asked Flower miserably.

"You are children – you have the strength of innocence."

"I don't understand," she began again, but he interrupted her with an impatient gesture.

"You'll go with Rikki Moon Shadow – you'll restore the spirit."

"How can *we* be of any use?" implored Brian.

"You can help us," he said. "You and Moon Shadow are untouched by greed. The theft is only a symptom of the Daiku's corruption. Only Rikki is untouched by the city and by the outside world." He paused. "You must help him. I shall pray to the condor that you will succeed." He vanished into the night before anything more could be said.

Shadows suddenly appeared from the trees. It was the Daiku – no longer passive and inert, but vigilant and angry. The noise of the storm had ceased and the heat seemed to close in on them. One of them stepped forward. He had something slumped in his arms.

Chief Mono also moved forward into the moonlight. He no longer seemed like a weak little man berating his tribe, but a figure of vengeance. How could Flower have ever felt that he was a crook, a liar, a fraud? thought Tim. He was clearly deeply shocked and enraged. Suddenly the young Daiku threw his burden to the ground in front of them. It was Rikki Moon Shadow, two darkly winking precious stones gripped in his hands.

"You came out of nowhere," said Chief Mono, "to take what you could. *He* brought you." He prised the stones out of Rikki's fingers and placed them reverently at the feet of the condor.

Rikki lay on the grass unconscious, the dried blood matted on his hair, while Flower, Brian and Tim stared at the Chief, unable to take in what he was saying. Their eyes kept reverting to the slumped figure. Was he alive? Tim was sure that he was breathing, but it was difficult to tell in the weak moonlight.

"I don't know what you're talking about," said Brian. "We haven't got anything to do with this. We couldn't have taken anything off the condor statue; we wouldn't have had time. Don't you remember – we were with you only a few minutes ago."

"Why did you come here?" asked Chief Mono accusingly.

"We were afraid that something would happen while you were down by the teepees," said Flower. "You'd left the statue unguarded."

"It was not unguarded," returned Mono abruptly. "We found two of our people in the bushes – unconscious. They've been badly hurt and have been taken to have their wounds dressed." There was a long silence, and then he continued: "Near them we found Rikki Moon Shadow, with our precious stones still grasped in his hands. He, too, was unconscious. Our people must have discovered him desecrating the shrine – perhaps ready to hand our sacred treasures over to his accomplices."

"Rubbish!" said Flower, but Chief Mono ignored her.

"Both our brothers are still unconscious; there is nothing they can tell us, but everything is obvious."

"No," said Flower. "It's not obvious."

"How can you accuse Rikki?" asked Tim. "Of all people, he's your greatest supporter. He cares more than anyone for the survival of the Daiku."

"The only people responsible for this are Ray Spark

and Lone Wolf," put in Brian. "Can't you see how they must have planned it all?"

"No," said a young man standing nearby. He had his arms round his wife, who was holding a sleepily gurgling baby close to her. "The evidence is all there. Moon Shadow has the precious stones in his hands."

"Perhaps it hasn't occurred to you," said Flower icily, "that Rikki may have been trying to rescue the stones."

"Chief Mono doesn't believe that," said the young man obstinately.

"No?"

"He knows Moon Shadow is guilty; and you – you're part of a gang which includes that man Spark and Lone Wolf – an organised gang. You've no idea how this has hurt Rikki's mother."

"Where is she?" asked Flower belligerently. "I want to talk to her."

"She is in her teepee," snapped Chief Mono, "too ashamed to come out and view her criminal son."

"You're making a mistake," said Flower, looking at the Daiku. "All of you. It's not —"

"Be quiet!" Mono clearly had no intention of letting her appeal to the tribe. "We have our own ways of dealing with thieves."

Tim looked down at Rikki. What were they going to do to them? He began to feel very afraid. Suddenly he saw Rikki's body stiffen and then, in a flash, he was on his feet. Green Watch hardly had time to register the fact that he had been faking a state of unconsciousness for the last few minutes when he yelled, "Come on!"

"Where?" stammered Brian.

"Follow me. We can outrun them. Now."

Still they hesitated as the Daiku began to close in on them.

"Come *on*! If you don't run we're finished. They'll tie you up in the open, and the nights are cold here. Very cold. Move!"

He began to run and they followed, while the Daiku, stung into action, surged towards them.

Keeping up with Rikki assured them of escape as he twisted and turned through the palm trees, but Tim was all too conscious that at least four of the younger tribespeople were close behind them in the darkness.

He stumbled and almost fell. Then he gathered himself together and ran as fast as he could, doubling his speed, his heart pumping. The canyon seemed desperately claustrophobic and the feeling of being hemmed in kept him going at twice his normal speed. Then, to his horror, he realised where Rikki was heading. They were out on the mountain again and the ground was rising sharply around them. He stared back for a moment and saw that two Indians, a young man and a woman, were close behind, running steadily and gaining all the time. If they carried on like this, Tim thought, with a chill dread stealing over him, he would soon be over the sheer drop again. He couldn't go on; he would rather be taken. There was no question about it – he couldn't run on that ridge again.

"Come *on*, Tim!" Suddenly Rikki was beside him; Flower and Brian were running ahead over the ridge, just as they had done earlier, maintaining a strong pace, showing no sign of fatigue.

"The ridge —"

"Come *on*!"

"I can't!"

"They're gaining."

"The drop – we'll be coming to the drop," gasped Tim. "I can't do it – I can't —"

"Run with me."

"You know I can't go on."

Rikki grasped Tim's arm in an iron grip. "*Run* with me!"

Reluctantly he did as he was told.

"Faster," Rikki urged. "They're close behind us now."

Tim picked up speed.

"Faster!"

He did the best he could, realising he had never run so fast before. Rikki's tight grip slackened, but it was still strong enough to urge him on, faster and faster, until his feet seemed to fly over the rising terrain. The sky was clearer now and the stars were like the bright jewels that had studded the condor.

"There she is!"

"What?"

"Look," said Rikki, his breathing even and without the slightest sign of flagging, "the condor."

She was there, hovering above them, her wings beating with no sign of any damage.

"She's OK," gasped Tim.

"Why shouldn't she be?"

"There was something wrong with her wing; we thought she'd been crippled."

"Maybe Lone Wolf grazed her. Perhaps he came close to —" Rikki broke off. "Come on, let's *really* run."

The condor was flying above them now, keeping pace with then – or were they keeping pace with her? Tim wasn't sure, but when he looked back he saw their pursuers were some distance away and they were slowly, but almost effortlessly, leaving them behind.

Again he had the odd sensation of flying, of his feet being centimetres off the ground. He looked down and realised that he and Rikki were now running over the ridge. He saw the drop that he had almost fallen into and loose boulders littering the gully below them.

"OK?" asked Rikki.

"I— yes."

And he was. He could have shouted aloud in exultation. The mountain, the vast canvas of sky, the desert below them, the sweet taste of the clean, dry cool air, and the running – the crazy, wonderful, effortless running with Rikki's arm linked in his – life was suddenly great. Could this have been the old Daiku way of life? With the condor flying above, bringing them all into a oneness of flight? For surely there was no doubt that the running had become flying. The best kept secret of all, said an exultant voice in Tim's mind; this was the spirit of the condor – of the Daiku – of wild lands which the alien settlers from the sea had never tamed.

"You're like braves," said Rikki proudly.

"Isn't that rather sexist?" panted Flower.

"Who said which sex braves were?" grinned Rikki.

They were sitting at the bottom of the mountain and the desert floor stretched ahead, seemingly into infinity, the landscape was sharply etched in the pallid moonlight.

"What happened to you?" asked Brian. "We thought you'd deserted us."

"When I heard that shot I was sure it was Lone Wolf. I had to find him to make sure. I had his trail once or twice but it petered out and I guessed he'd left the canyon. I was climbing these mountains when I saw them coming in – Spark, Lone Wolf and half a dozen men I'd never seen before. They looked like a lot of heavies to me. I followed them and then headed them off, and got to the shrine at least five minutes before they showed up."

He paused until they couldn't bear it any longer. "Well?" asked Tim in desperation. "What happened next?"

Rikki went on. "I saw both of the guards lying unconscious, then a figure crouching in the undergrowth. I went after it, but it slipped away and I walked into a trap. Chief Mono's trap."

"So he *was* involved," breathed Flower.

"He'd really taken me in," said Rikki bitterly. "For years he'd taken me in. He hit me with some kind of club as I came round a tree and I went down. I caught a glimpse of his face as I fell, but I'm sure he didn't realise that or he would have killed me." He spoke softly, but with tremendous conviction. "Then he must have put those stones in my hands to incriminate me."

"Who is he?" asked Flower. "Is he really a member of the tribe?"

"Yes. He went away and came back, like most of us."

"Where did he go?"

"To L.A. Where else? I think he worked as an odd job man in a hotel. What other opportunities do we guys get? But he's been back for years – maybe ten. He took over the leadership when his father died – it's always been the tradition for his family to lead."

"Did you trust him?" asked Brian.

"Yes."

"No doubts about him at all?"

"I never really got on with him. He lived the tribal life, managed the things we sell, believed in the things we believe in, but I always felt there was a gulf between us – that he was a dry stick of a man. I couldn't feel any real involvement – any passion in him. But there are plenty of others like that."

"So why did he decide to do it now?" asked Tim.

"Maybe he's been biding his time all these years," Rikki said brusquely. "Waiting for someone else to come back from the city who felt like he did."

"Like Lone Wolf?" whispered Tim.

"Yes, like Lone Wolf. Someone who felt as disassociated as he did, but someone who wasn't just prepared to wait and dream."

"And both of them were waiting for someone like Spark," said Brian. "Just a big Spark to get the whole thing going."

"Are you *sure* he's involved?" asked Tim, remembering how Spark had saved his life and the gentle way he had talked him down. Surely there could be some mistake?

But Rikki ignored him. "They've been waiting a long time," he said, "Mono and Lone Wolf. Maybe they even regret what they've done, which is more than someone like Spark would. But greed won out in the end."

"What do we do now?" asked Tim. It was so good to have Rikki back with them again that any future danger seemed diminished. Glancing across at Flower and Brian he guessed they felt very much the same. He was still disturbed about Spark, but decided not to say any more – at least for the moment.

"I'm going after him," said Rikki.

"Correction," said Flower. "We all are. We spoke to the dream-keeper – it's what *he* wanted."

"Look —"

"Rikki, you've deserted us once. We won't let you out of our sight again."

"It's too dangerous – the dream-keeper's old. He doesn't —"

"Rubbish!" She was adamant. "You know what

we've done in the past. We can help you," she snapped.

"Your father would —"

"Approve," she said sternly. "You know he would."

Rikki sighed. "Maybe he would," he agreed unwillingly.

"Do you know where they might have taken the stones?" asked Flower. "If they're not still lurking around here, that is."

"They won't hang around," replied Rikki firmly. "I could hazard a guess as to where they've gone: an island a few kilometres off the coast – the one that used to be owned by the Rush family."

"Who does it belong to now?"

"Dinah Rush," Rikki said quietly. "And if Dinah's in on this, we've got big trouble. She's dynamite."

"Are you sure they'd take the stones there?" asked Brian after a long, tense silence.

Rikki shrugged. "It's a reasonable guess. The island would be a good place to hide out."

"How are we going to get them back?" asked Brian bleakly. "They've probably got a load of hired heavies out there."

"I'm going to see someone I trust – I'd like you all to come with me."

"Who's that?" asked Flower nervously. Tim guessed that she was feeling they could hardly trust anyone now – not after Chief Mono.

"His name is Coyote; he's a recluse."

"An Indian?"

"A Daiku. But he prefers to live alone. He taught me how to run."

"But how can he help us?" asked Tim.

"I don't know that he can. But he's my friend: he's been like a father to me and I have to see him before we go back to the ocean."

"Where does he live?"

"Over there. By the rocks."

They stared into the desert and saw a vague, insubstantial shape. It looked a long distance away.

"The condor's gone," said Brian suddenly, looking around him.

"She'll turn up again," said Rikki casually. He rose to his feet. "I think she recognises me, and I'm pretty sure she'll follow. She's more than good luck."

"Yes," said Flower. "She's definitely more than that."

"Let's go," said Rikki. "Coyote will be able to give us food and shelter. Then, when we've had a rest, we can start off at dawn." He paused. "I have to tell you something."

"Well?" asked Flower suspiciously, as if she feared he was trying to get rid of them again.

"I'm glad you're coming with me," he said. "You're not like kids. You're like – I don't know – like a source of great strength."

The three members of Green Watch had never felt so pleased in their lives.

Chapter Eight

The rock was much further away than they had imagined, and trekking to it over the desert floor took a couple of hours. The air was cold, but Tim soon found that if he really kept moving he was warm enough. As he walked in the dry night he kept thinking about Ray Spark and the way he had saved his life. At first he had been quite unable to believe that Spark was a villain, and although he was now beginning to accept that he must be involved in some way, he was still reluctant to condemn Spark before he knew for certain that he had helped to steal the precious stones of the Daiku.

Eventually they drew closer to the vast shadow of the rock and Flower said despondently, "I don't see anyone."

"You will – look for his fire."

As they approached, Tim could see a crevice to one side of the rock and a small, welcoming fire flickering inside. After another ten minutes they were there, clambering over the uneven surface to the fire, a jeep and a small hut. But there still seemed to be no one around.

"Coyote!" whispered Rikki. "Coyote!"

The muzzle of a rifle appeared from behind the hut.

"It's me, Rikki."

The rifle was lowered and an Indian, somewhere in his late fifties, stepped into view. He had long black hair tumbling down to his shoulders and large dark eyes. Even in the night, Tim could almost feel his gaze boring into him.

"There's trouble," said Rikki.

"Yes." Coyote didn't sound in the least surprised.

"The shrine's been desecrated."

"I wondered when that would happen." His voice was deep but rusty-sounding, as if he hardly ever used it, and he seemed to choose his words carefully, speaking slowly and weighing each one. He gestured towards the fire and they crouched around the flames gratefully. "The tribe have been living too long in the material world," he added reflectively.

"That's why you moved away, isn't it?" asked Brian shrewdly.

"There is a wonderful life to be led out here," said Coyote, looking up at the stars. "But the Daiku had become too aware of modern times for that life to be

79

preserved. You have to be at one with the elements. Once we could do that together, but not any more."

"We tried." Rikki was defensive.

"Yes," replied Coyote gently. "It was a good try. I gave up – I was too selfish." He looked around him. "But at least I have all this, and it's still here."

"I'm not going to let the Daiku die," said Rikki. "I'm going to get the jewels back from the city."

"They'll be contaminated," spat out Coyote. "It'll happen all over again. And you'll have to keep the shrine under lock and key."

"I don't know what we'll do with it; outsiders could come and take it." Rikki paused. "Even if we manage to protect it from the public, we can't protect it from ourselves. We'd have to learn to trust each other."

"The Daiku are like the condor," said Coyote. "Both have become endangered species."

"It began in the city," said Rikki, but Coyote shrugged.

"It began when we lost the purity – the wonderment of it all." His face was sad. Then he became more matter-of-fact. "Do you know who is responsible for the theft?"

"It was partly the work of an outsider who – contaminated two of the tribe," said Rikki hesitantly.

Coyote spoke curtly. "Weren't they corrupt already?"

Rikki sighed. "Some."

"How many?"

"To our knowledge, two."

"*Our* knowledge?" For the first time, Coyote's

large, liquid eyes ranged over Green Watch. "Who are these children?"

"They're members of an environmental group called Green Watch. And yes, maybe they're kids, but they've really proved themselves to me."

Coyote nodded. "That is enough then. Rikki Moon Shadow is a unique example of a Daiku who can go into the city and remain unscathed, untainted. There are not many like that." Then, without giving them a chance to reply, he turned back to Rikki and asked, "The Daiku – who are they?"

"Lone Wolf. He has been in L.A. for years and has only recently come back."

"That's predictable enough."

"And Mono."

There was a long silence. For a few moments Coyote closed his eyes, and when he opened them again, Tim could see that there were tears in them.

"He was my friend," he muttered. "I trusted him."

"He's been back from the city for many years," said Rikki.

"Yes."

"But perhaps he'd lost what you were saying – the purity of tribal living. Maybe it all went sour on him."

Rikki began to describe exactly what had happened and then what they were going to do. When he had finished, Coyote, a deep pain in his dark eyes, asked quietly, "And the condor?"

81

"She's around. We saw her a while ago when we were on our way to you."

He smiled. "She's here." He made a clucking sound through his teeth and the bird slowly appeared from round the back of the hut. Her red head and neck, her dark, richly plumed body and white feet looked spectral and mysterious in the moonlight. To Tim's surprise she nuzzled up to Coyote, pushing her beak into the loose folds of his moccasin jacket. "I dressed her wound. It was only a graze – the slightest of grazes."

"You mean she came to you?" asked Brian in amazement.

"Yes. She comes here regularly, ever since she was very young."

"Couldn't you have a try at mating her with a male in captivity?" asked Flower.

"Or would that be like bringing one of the Daiku back from the city and into Palm Canyon?" asked Brian shrewdly.

"No," said Coyote. "I've already been approached by a naturalist about mating the condor, but Chief Mono was against the idea. Now I realise he hoped the tribe might disperse if the condor died out, and then it would have been easier to get at the stones."

"Yes," said Rikki bitterly. "It's all beginning to add up."

Coyote nodded. "We're hanging on to shreds of our lives: the canyon, the tribe, the condor —" Then he spoke on a firmer note. "So, tell me what you're going to do."

"I reckon the precious stones have been taken to a small island called Serendipity; just off Coronado. It was owned by the Rush family, but they're all dead now except for Dinah – Ray Spark's girlfriend. Anyway, it'll be our first pitch."

"We mustn't forget the safety of the condor," said Coyote. He continued, his voice shaking with emotion. "You *have* to realise, all of you, that the condor is in deadly danger."

"From Spark?" asked Flower. "He won't be around here any longer."

"From the whole tribe," replied Coyote sharply.

"But why?"

"Now that the shrine is gone," said Rikki, "our belief tells us that the condor will leave us. Forever. But there's something else," he stared at Coyote miserably. "Some of the Daiku believe that Lone Wolf is dead, and that his spirit is inhabiting the condor's body."

Coyote sighed and Tim said involuntarily, "These people – quite a lot of them anyway – have lived in Los Angeles. Will they be able to believe in the old ways again?"

"Once you're back in Palm Canyon you soon slip back to a different way of life – a different set of beliefs. Things happen— that don't happen in cities. I can't explain it any other way."

"Yes," said Flower unexpectedly. "I can see that."

Brian said nothing and Tim wondered what he felt. As for himself, he didn't know what to think. Anything seemed possible out here in the enormity of the desert, which had remained unchanged for so many thousands of years.

"Whatever you believe," said Coyote gently, "we all have to accept that the condor is in very great danger. It would be better if she stayed with me."

Rikki nodded in agreement. "How can you persuade her to stay?" he began, but Coyote interrupted him.

"I can't force her to do anything." He turned back to Green Watch. "She may follow you to Serendipity."

"Why should she do that?" asked Tim.

"Another belief you may doubt or perhaps accept." Coyote smiled for the first time. "The condor will follow those in peril."

"And will she guard them?" asked Flower.

"The condor does as she chooses," he replied quickly.

That's not much good, thought Tim.

"She's neither a guardian nor an avenger," continued Coyote. "She is simply the spirit of the Daiku."

"If she comes with us," said Brian, "anything could happen to her."

"Yes."

"Well, don't you think —"

"She *has* to face danger. A condor hovered over many of the battles the Daiku had with American troops. It was a tradition."

Many of those battles were lost, weren't they? thought Tim. Then he remembered Custer's last stand. Maybe not all.

Rikki looked at his watch. "We must leave at dawn," he said. "And it's almost two in the morning."

"Will you eat?" asked Coyote.

Suddenly all three members of Green Watch remembered how desperately hungry they were.

Curled up in soft blankets on the floor of Coyote's hut, having eaten plate after plate of delicious soup, Tim fell into an immediate deep sleep. He dreamt all four of them were embarking on a long journey across the desert towards the ocean. The condor was there too, swooping high above them, wheeling up and over the moon. She was covered in diamonds which winked and twinkled against the stars. The long, straight, dusty road in front of them stretched out endlessly. There were no mountains, only a long thin finger of rock that shot menacingly towards the sky. It was jet black granite and on its narrow peak stood Ray Spark, rifle upraised, following the flight of the condor. On ledges either side of him, a little lower down, stood Chief Mono and Lone Wolf, also with upraised rifles. All three looked like toy warriors until they began to fire. Tim raced towards them as fast he could, but in true dream style the sand became mud and he found himself sinking up to the waist.

"Stop!" he yelled. "Don't kill the condor!"

But Ray Spark didn't even turn round. As Tim continued shouting, Spark said in a distant voice, "You owe me a favour, son."

"I owe you my life!" screamed Tim.

"I'll take the condor's," he replied, laughing, and fired again.

The condor tumbled down in a heap of bloodied feathers, covering Tim as he sank further into the mud. He struggled desperately, unable to breathe, and then woke, wrestling with the blankets.

"You OK?" asked Flower.

"Eh?"

"You've been dreaming."

"Yes," he muttered.

"So, are you OK?"

Tim nodded. But he wasn't. He was afraid, more afraid than he had ever been in his life before. In the past Green Watch's battles had been with reality, but he knew that this time not only was he trying to save the condor and all she represented, but he was up against belief as well, and a very alien belief at that. He looked up at Flower and then at Rikki and Brian still sleeping. Were they strong enough? he wondered. Somehow they had to be.

An hour later they were being driven over the desert by Coyote in his beat-up old jeep, which lurched and spluttered and heaved its way over the rocky surface of the road. Flower had questioned its usefulness when they had first set out. "Don't you find it's a reminder of all the mechanical things that helped destroy the Indian way of life?"

Coyote had sighed. "In a way you're right, but I need to patrol the desert – find out what's going on. I don't want anyone creeping up on my rock, stealing my things, maybe trying to lay some kind of claim on where I live. So," he had shrugged, "I've had to go along with the age of transport."

After a couple of hours' driving, Coyote stopped and pointed up at the condor wheeling above them.

"I'll run with her for a bit. She feels reassured that way. You drive for a while, Rikki."

Fascinated, they watched him dismount and begin to jog beside the road. Then Coyote started to run and the condor swooped low over his head, its wings beating strongly, matching his easy, loping strides by the side of the desert highway.

"He certainly can go!" said Rikki, speeding up the rattling jeep. "He's really covering the ground."

"So Coyote taught you to run," said Flower.

"Yeah, but I'll never be as fast as he is."

No one could, thought Tim, for Coyote's feet hardly seemed to touch the ground. It was really amazing to see the man and the bird pacing each other, neither of them young, yet both free and joyous in the early morning.

Eventually Coyote slowed down and the condor flew lower, dipping its wings as if in greeting. Then Coyote jumped into the jeep. He was hardly out of breath at all as he watched the bird climb higher and higher into the sky.

"It began with the discovery," Coyote muttered. "And it'll end with us all in the cities, unless we're careful," he added.

"Discovery?" asked Brian.

"Of America. Columbus and all that. Or Cristobal Colón, to get his name right," said Coyote. "When the white man came to our shores, he took everything."

"If we can get the stones back," said Rikki, "we'll rebuild the shrine. Then we'll re-establish our laws and eventually I'll get our lands back." He paused, looking at Coyote for a moment and then turning back to the wheel. "I suppose you must think I'm just an idealist." He laughed awkwardly.

"Perhaps," said Coyote. "But I wish you well. Maybe – not maybe, for sure – you're the Daiku's only chance. You and Green Watch." He looked up again at the condor. "Maybe she'll go with you," he said. "But if she does, try and look after her."

"We'll try," said Rikki. "Of course we'll try." There was enormous conviction in his voice, but Tim knew how hard the task ahead was going to be. Would they really be able to protect the condor as well?

But Flower was even more committed than Rikki. "We'll not let *anyone* harm her," she said passionately.

He took her hand suddenly and gently kissed her finger-tips. "It's belief that will save her," he said. "Belief as strong as yours."

Chapter Nine

They set off for Serendipity Island just after lunch in Rikki's motor-boat. The sea was rough with a strong wind blowing and they bounced over the waves, spray flying.

"It's not far offshore," said Rikki. "No one goes there now. It used to be run as a nature reserve, but old man Rush died years ago and the old lady last year." He paused. "Of course the place is overrun by dogs." He sounded as if he were ashamed of not telling them before – as if he had been deliberately withholding the knowledge from them.

"Dogs? What kind of dogs?" asked Brian uneasily.

"Alsatians. She used to breed them."

"Who looks after them now?"

"A caretaker – an old woman naturalist who still lives out there."

There was a long pause, and then Flower said, "Do the alsatians run wild?"

Rikki looked at her uneasily. "There are notices up all over the island about them and forbidding anyone to land." Somehow he didn't sound as confident out here at sea as he had on land.

Tim glanced at Brian and Flower. "Where are you going to land?" he asked.

"There's an overgrown inlet on the west side. We'll go for that."

An hour later, they began to approach Serendipity, which looked like a mass of dense and sinister vegetation. It seemed to have no beach, and creepers trailed into the water like clutching tentacles.

"What a dump!" said Brian.

But there was more to it than that, thought Tim. The place seemed to be waiting for them, ready to ensnare them in its dusty-looking thickets. Tim shivered. Was he just suffering from lack of sleep and an over-worked imagination?

"There's a house, and some outbuildings on the other side," said Rikki. "And a landing stage. The whole place is only about a kilometre wide." He pulled out a pair of binoculars and stared at the coastline. "No sign of life," he whispered.

They pulled the boat up amongst the suffocating foliage around the inlet and paused to review the situation.

"We'll keep together," said Rikki. "Whatever you do, don't get separated."

"Are we going to explore the whole island?" asked Brian.

"No. I think we should just make for the old house." He paused, staring at a palm tree near the shore. "Hang on. Look at that tree."

He began to walk towards it when Brian yelled out, "Stop!"

"What's going on?"

"Freeze!"

"This a joke?" asked Rikki.

"I said – freeze." Brian's voice was unsteady. "Don't move." Tim craned to look at Rikki's feet. All he could see was what looked like a long piece of wire.

"What is it?" Rikki was taking him seriously now.

"I don't know if I'm right, but there's wire – just a fraction away from your foot. Suppose it triggers something off?" Brian was sweating with sudden, insistent fear.

Tim felt nausea rising from the pit of his stomach as Rikki began to edge away from the wire.

"Don't move," said Brian. "Please don't move."

"You think I'm going to stand here all day?"

"I just *know* there's something there."

"How?"

"I've read books about explosives and mines and things." Brian's voice trembled childishly.

Tim didn't know what to say. He knew that Brian wanted to be a scientist and was always reading textbooks. Maybe he was right. Then he thought of something Rikki had said a few minutes earlier. "The tree," he said. "What did you say was on the tree?"

"An Indian sign – I'm just trying to make out what it says. Yeah, it reads: LOOK INTO THE TREES WITH BRIGHT EYES."

"What on earth —" began Tim, but Rikki was still speaking.

"The sign – see this sign – it means danger. And then the message." He paused and looked down at the wire again. "I guess —"

"Stay there!" Brian had moved a few paces forward and had suddenly gone down on his hands and knees, gently raking aside the sand with his fingers.

"Be careful. For God's sake —"

Tim looked up intuitively. The condor was overhead, a black speck against the sun. "The condor's here," he whispered.

Brian was still pushing the sand aside gently, working his way round Rikki and towards the trees. Gradually the wire was exposed.

"Please, Brian," hissed Flower.

"I'm OK." The sweat was pouring into his eyes. "Let me go on." Agonisingly he went on pushing the sand gently aside until he began to work his way uphill. Then he paused. "It's attached to something."

"Don't go any further," said Tim.

"I don't understand why —"

"Leave it, Brian." Rikki's voice was hoarse.

"I'll just uncover this last bit."

"Brian!" yelled Flower.

"No," said Tim. "No."

Slowly Brian was exposing a large cylindrical object with more wire attached to it. As he did so, Rikki suddenly gave a great bark of laughter.

"OK." He moved out of position, stepping on the wire as he did so.

"What are you doing?" shouted Brian. He flattened himself on the ground. The others threw themselves down instinctively, but Rikki remained standing. He laughed again, good-naturedly and with enormous relief.

"It's OK."

"Eh?" Tim lifted his head from the sand.

"It's an old cable drum, just a roll of cable, that's all."

"Thank God." Flower got to her feet, leaving Brian on the sand, staring up at Rikki in disbelief.

"You mean —" he began.

"It's a false alarm."

Brian got slowly to his feet amidst a self-conscious silence. Tim struggled to find something to say - anything to prevent one of his dearest friends from looking a fool. But his mind went a total blank and he couldn't think of anything to say at all. It was Rikki who saved the situation. He went straight across to Brian, put his arm round him and said, "Well done!"

"Are you sure it's only —"

"Yeah. I'm sure."

"I'm sorry." There were tears in Brian's eyes and Tim couldn't bear to watch.

"Listen, you did a brilliant job." Rikki was determined to boost his morale – to stop him breaking down.

"Rubbish!"

"But you did. It's being so alert that counts."

"I feel a complete idiot."

"Maybe you do, but I could have been dead."

"Could have been." Brian brushed a hand across his eyes. "Oh, yes – *could* have been."

"Come on, Brian." Rikki's voice was calm and reasonable. "You've got to realise what a valuable warning you gave all of us."

"Don't patronise me," he replied savagely, pulling away from Rikki.

"I'm not."

"Brian," said Flower, "you did really well."

"You're more observant than any of us." At last Tim had found something to say. But it didn't go down very well.

"I *said* – don't patronise me." Brian was still furious, with them and with himself.

Then Flower stiffened. "What was that?"

"I didn't hear anything," said Tim abruptly.

"I thought I heard a dog barking," she said.

"We'd better push on," said Rikki.

Brian looked down miserably, unable to meet anyone's eye. He'll get over it, thought Tim. He's bound to. It'll just take a bit of time.

"Stay where you are!" Brian suddenly rapped out.

Rikki turned, grinning. "Glad you can take a joke, Brian."

"I'm not taking a joke, you idiot!"

"What?"

"There's something stretched across the track."

"I can't see anything. Brian, is this —"

"No. Use your eyes. It's so thin you can hardly see it."

"Where?"

"Ankle level, Look!"

"I can see it," said Flower suddenly. "It's there." She grabbed Tim, pointing. Finally, he could make out what she meant. You'd need very keen eyesight to spot it, but that was what Brian had always had.

Rikki paused. "Move back," he said. "All of you."

They walked back, almost into the sea.

"You're vindicated, Brian," he said.

"Thanks." But there was no cynicism, only pleasure in his voice.

"OK." Rikki picked up a stone. "Time for target practice. Get back into the sea."

Dutifully they moved back into the warm, lapping water while Rikki shied the stone. It hit the wire and nothing happened.

"Nice shot," said Tim.

"Needs to be harder." He picked up a larger stone and tried again. Still nothing happened. Then he grabbed at a small rock and threw it with all his

95

might. Again nothing happened. Rikki walked swiftly towards the wire.

"What are you doing?" asked Brian.

"If a stone won't operate it, maybe this will." There was a huge piece of wood lying in the bushes. Staggering, Rikki picked it up and hurled it against the wire. For a moment they all stood there expectantly. Then there was a cracking sound as a tree crashed down over the path, followed by another from the opposite side.

"Was the cable something to do with it?" asked Flower. "Something to do with the trap?"

"No, just old stuff, rotting away on the beach," said Rikki. "Maybe it was used to secure boats. It's the other stuff – the much thinner wire – that was the trap. Thank God you spotted it, Brian."

"But the notice," said Flower. "It's ludicrous."

"It's recent," replied Rikki.

"If they could warn us, why couldn't they remove it?"

"No idea. It's a tricky one. These two trees were sawn by an expert – just far enough to leave them standing. If the weight of a human being walked into the wire, it would be enough to bring them down." He turned to Brian. "I don't know how many of us it would have killed."

But Brian was barely listening. "Be quiet!" he said abruptly.

"What's the matter?" whispered Tim, fear gripping him again.

"Dogs," he said. "I'm sure of it."

They began to push their way through the dense foliage about fifty metres down from the trap until eventually they came to a dark, dusty clearing.

"Do you think they know we're coming?" asked Tim, as they paused for breath.

"I don't know," said Rikki. "I don't even know whether the trees were prepared for us, or someone else, or anyone. It seems a very elaborate trap just for the odd trespasser."

"Who else would come after the stones?" asked Flower.

"Once they're known to be missing every crook who can find his way down the San Diego Highway," said Rikki.

As he spoke, they again heard the sound of barking; it didn't seem so far away this time, but there was a curious muffled resonance to it, as if the dogs were shut away somewhere. Tim felt slightly more reassured.

"I reckon they're inside," said Rikki. "Maybe in a cellar. So I suggest we move fast before someone gets the idea of letting them out."

"Have you got a plan of action?" asked Flower doubtfully.

"No," said Rikki, giving her a reckless grin.

"Look —" Rikki stopped and parted some huge dusty leaves. They had moved on from the clearing and were hacking their way through dense foliage when suddenly it all petered out. "It was a lawn once," he said. They crowded silently round him to peer ahead, and saw what looked like a field of high grass and weeds that threatened to engulf a crumbling old white clapboard mansion. The house looked very run down, and shutters covered most of the windows except a couple of small ones on the ground floor.

"I won't get through those," said Rikki.

"I will," said Tim. "I'm the smallest."

"You're not going in there alone," said Brian crisply.

"I may have to."

"No way," said Flower. "Isn't that right, Rikki?"

"We go everywhere together," he said gravely. "Everywhere."

A few minutes later, Tim was squeezing his way through one of the small downstairs windows. He had finally won the argument, for when they had checked right round the old house, there had been no sign of habitation or movement at all – not even a bark, so the dogs must be kept somewhere else. The only sign of human activity was flattened grass leading from the opposite side of the clearing to the front door. They had tried every other window and the other doors, but all were locked and shuttered, and it was only the smallest of the windows that Rikki managed to prise open.

Before Tim had gone in, however, a whispered argument had taken place.

"It's too dangerous," Flower had insisted.

"Anyone could be in there," Brian had pronounced.

"And we're not splitting up," Rikki had put in.

But Tim had won them round, promising to keep returning to the window every five minutes or so.

Inside, the house was sparsely furnished and full of grime and cobwebs. He checked the living room and a small scullery and was just about to walk into the kitchen when he paused, sure that he had heard something, although he couldn't quite identify the sound. What was it? A kind of purring? Hissing? Or was it heavy breathing? Tim crept forward.

Carefully, cautiously, silently pushing open the door, Tim tried to make out the shape in front of him. At first it just looked like a heap of old clothes, and then he realised with a shock that what he was looking at was someone slumped in a chair with their wrists tied. The sound he had heard was the prisoner's harsh and ragged breathing.

Tim looked around him and then tiptoed on, feeling sick with apprehension. He came round to face the prisoner and peered into the dark face of a young Indian whose mouth was sealed by tape which almost covered his nose as well. No wonder he was having such a struggle to breathe. With a quick movement, Tim ripped the tape away, and with a sharp cry the Indian's eyes fastened on his own in mingled pain and relief.

"Who are you?" asked Tim.

"Lone Wolf," came the hoarse reply.

"*Lone Wolf*?"

"Yes."

"But I thought —"

"You thought right. I helped Spark take the stones," said Lone Wolf frankly.

"Then why did he tie you up like this?" asked Tim suspiciously.

"I'd had enough. I saw the condor hovering overhead. I knew I'd done a terrible thing."

"Did you make the trap?" Tim sounded very doubtful, for he found it hard to accept anything Lone Wolf was saying.

"The trees? Spark made me set it; that inlet's the only other way into Serendipity, apart from the jetty. But I put the Indian sign up, hoping Rikki would see it."

"He did," replied Tim.

"Thank God!" Lone Wolf burst out. "Spark offered me a lot of money to help him pull this off."

"Was it the condor that changed your mind?" asked Tim with the same suspicion.

"It's what the condor represents – the old life I threw away when I went to L.A. The strange thing is that when I got back I loved the canyon, the Daiku, everything they stood for. But I was always so restless. I kept thinking – is this it? Is this all it's ever going to be? So when Spark approached me and talked about the kind of money I could get out of this, I jumped at the chance." He paused. "But directly I left the canyon I knew what I'd done – how much I'd left behind. Seeing the condor clinched it for me."

Tim stared hard into Lone Wolf's eyes. There was something about the way he was speaking now that was utterly convincing. "Who else is here?" he asked, suddenly conscious of time passing too quickly.

"Spark and Dinah Rush. She's the force behind all this – that lady's got twice Spark's strength."

"Where are they?"

"Down at the boathouse, waiting for Chief Mono to come over with the guy who's going to buy the stones."

"Did you try to get away?"

"Yeah. I almost got to the boat, but they set the dogs on me and it was lucky those brutes didn't savage me to death. Dinah called them off."

"Why?" asked Tim.

"Maybe she won't go so far as killing – I don't know. She's a very unpredictable lady. Get this wretched rope off – I've got to move. Fast."

Tim began to struggle to untie him. "Where are the dogs?" he asked urgently. Could he trust Lone Wolf? He'd have to.

"In the boathouse."

Tim looked quickly at his watch and then hurriedly untied the last of Lone Wolf's bonds. It was time for him to go back to the window to reassure the others. "How can we trust you?" he asked.

"You can't," said Lone Wolf bleakly. "But you need me," he added, rubbing at his wrists and shakily standing up. "I've been here for hours," he muttered.

"How are you going to get out? I squeezed in through one of those little windows."

"I'll get the back door open and we'll go out together." Then he paused and cursed. "We'll trample down more grass. We'll have to go out the front way and pray no one sees us."

"It didn't look as if there was anyone around," said Tim. "And the others are monitoring everything." Suddenly he remembered something. "But there's a naturalist here somewhere, isn't there? A woman who studies birds?"

Lone Wolf shook his head. "I've never seen her. Maybe they've shut her up like me. Come on. Let's go."

They took some time to unlock the heavy chain and bolts on the front door and finally, cautiously, to open it. There was no one around and the late afternoon sun was mellow and welcoming. Just beyond the tangle of undergrowth, he could hear the Pacific murmuring innocently. The stillness seemed impenetrable, as if time were suspended.

"Rikki will get a terrible shock when he sees me," said Lone Wolf. "Let's hope he doesn't just kill me on the spot."

Chapter Ten

"What on earth —?" Rikki clenched a fist and moved forward ferociously.

"No," said Tim. "He's OK."

"*What?*"

Flower and Brian stared at Tim as if he were mad.

"He's changed."

"Don't you believe him!" snapped Rikki.

"Honestly. I found him tied up."

"You should have left him that way."

"Please," said Lone Wolf desperately. "He's right. I saw the condor."

"You tried to kill her," said Rikki, unimpressed, looking at the Indian with hatred in his eyes.

"Yes. But it's a miracle – she's flying again."

"As usual your shooting was lousy. Coyote fixed her up."

"Yeah. I guessed that's what might have happened. Anyway, I saw her flying over the island, and I just realised what a fool I'd been."

"He means what he says." Tim was adamant.

"Yeah, but for how long?" Rikki remained solidly unimpressed. "You don't believe in the Daiku."

"I do now," said Lone Wolf quietly. "And this time I won't change. But I can't prove it to you, Rikki. Not at the moment I can't."

"I haven't the slightest faith in you, so one false move and you're finished. Understood?" said Rikki contemptuously.

"Understood."

"So where are Spark and Rush?"

"They're down by the boathouse. There's a cabin there."

"What are they doing?"

"Waiting for Chief Mono and some guy he's bringing along to take the stones."

"When?"

"Soon."

"OK. Let's go," said Rikki. "And remember, don't step out of line. Not for one moment."

"Maybe you should remember something," said Lone Wolf. "Something you've overlooked, Rikki."

"What?"

"The dogs. Dinah has a dozen alsatians down there. They used to belong to her mother. They're old but vicious, and I would guess she's keeping them hungry."

"I'm not overlooking them," snapped Rikki. Suddenly he looked exhausted, drained of energy. "We heard them barking."

Cautiously the five of them struggled back into the long undergrowth and began to trek towards the shore. There was no sound but the clicking of grasshoppers, which seemed to intensify as they moved painfully through the thickets. Lone Wolf walked just in front of Rikki, with the others strung out behind. Tim felt very tense, but they had been through so much together that there was a kind of reassurance in numbers; hunting as a pack, he thought. The word pack remained in his mind as they pushed their way through the dusty tangled thickets as quietly as possible. Then Brian stopped and hissed at Lone Wolf and Rikki, "Stop!"

"What gives?"

"I think I heard something."

They listened in total silence and then Tim heard the sound as well and began to tremble as he realised grimly that the panting was all around them. They were surrounded.

Flower was the first to spot an alsatian. "There!"

The dog lay half concealed in the undergrowth, its tongue hanging out, its eyes narrowed to dark, cruel little specks. Slowly, lethargically, other dogs moved in.

"Just walk on," said Rikki.

"Where?" asked Lone Wolf.

Rikki gazed wildly around, but it was Tim who saw the tree house about fifty metres away.

"Look over there! And isn't that a ladder on the side?"

"Well done, Tim. Everyone take it easy. Walk slowly. Be unconcerned. Don't look at them; just keep going."

Tim remembered all too well their recent contact with a gorilla in Africa and how, despite being warned not to, Brian's eyes had been irrevocably drawn to those of the animal.* Now Tim felt the same, as if he could not walk through the ring without making contact with at least one watchful eye.

When they had moved only a few metres, the growling began. It came from very deep within the animals' throats and sounded terrifying. Tim forced his eyes down on the ground and almost bumped into a palm tree. His strangled cry of shock seemed to make the alsatians' growling descend to a deeper note.

"Shut up!" hissed Rikki.

"Sorry."

"Keep going. Don't hurry, whatever you do."

Tim felt the sanctuary of the tree house was a lifetime away. He had to keep looking up to see where he was going, and felt his eyes literally dragged towards the bloodshot pupils of one particularly huge

* Gorilla Mountain

alsatian. Gradually the dog rose to its feet and moved closer, hackles rising, and Tim felt consumed by unbearable panic. Sweat ran into his eyes and he longed desperately to break into a run.

After what seemed like hours, they arrived at the bottom of the tree house ladder and the blessed sanctuary it offered.

"I'll stand here," said Rikki. "You go up. Make it slow and steady. No sudden movements or noise."

They did as he told them – Brian, then Flower and then Tim. But when Tim was only a few metres off the ground one of the dogs sprang and he felt its hot, foetid breath near the back of his neck. Fortunately the animal just missed him and rolled back on the ground. Immediately the growling died away and raucous barking began. It's all up now, thought Tim as he hauled himself up to the platform at the top. Any minute Spark will come running.

"Get up there," said Rikki to Lone Wolf. "Get up there fast."

"I'm not hanging around, man!"

He was up the ladder in seconds, while the pack of alsatians stood round Rikki, barking monotonously. "Get away!" he yelled, picking up a stick. The dogs cringed back momentarily.

Where's the condor? wondered Tim, but when he looked up through the fine tracery of branches the sky was empty.

Then Rikki threw himself at the ladder and was up it in seconds, as one alsatian after another hurled itself as far up as it could. Once he was on the platform, the dogs leapt and reared, barking more loudly and ferociously than ever, but for a moment Tim felt a sense of triumph. The dogs had been fooled. Then he realised they were trapped.

The tree house was quite a substantial structure and made Tim think of the Swiss Family Robinson. Looking up, he could see that it was built on two levels: one set of rooms on their level and another further up the branches. From his vantage point he could see into a large, airy kitchen with a rocking chair, a table and a butane gas stove. There was a dresser with cups and plates arranged on it and a larder that was wide open, with tins, bread, fruit and vegetables. Hunger pangs began to bite but they faded quickly when he heard the sound of feet on the platform above him. Then a pair of bare feet followed by long tapering legs began to descend the ladder and a voice said, "Just what do you think you folks are doing?"

The woman was wearing a cool linen dress, and when her face eventually appeared, she turned out to be good looking in a spare, out-of-doors way. She must have been in her forties, with a mop of auburn hair, and freckles which even stood out on a nut-brown face. Meanwhile, below them the alsatians changed their barking to a long-drawn-out howling.

"Don't you know what's going on here?" said Rikki incredulously.

"I mind my own business," she replied sharply.

"You know the owners?"

"Miss Dinah? She lets me live here, doing the job I want to do. In peace!" she added threateningly.

"And the dogs?"

"Someone's upset them."

"You don't say," said Lone Wolf sarcastically. "They're starving."

The woman ignored his comment, saying: "They're usually my responsibility, but since Miss Dinah's been back, she's taken them over."

"You don't think they look a little hungry?" repeated Lone Wolf.

"Perhaps you could tell me what you're doing in my home."

Rikki laughed hollowly. "We didn't have too much choice —" He looked down at the still baying dogs.

"The island's private," she exclaimed. "You've no right to be here."

"Ray Spark has stolen some property that belongs to the Daiku. I want the stuff back, and that's why we're here. Now, are you going to help or not?" He stared at her impatiently.

"I don't believe a word of all this."

"You'll have to start trying," said Rikki grimly.

She looked at him in disbelief. "It all sounds mighty strange." Then her eyes fastened on the dogs and she began to talk to them quietly. Gradually the howling stopped and the dogs began to slink away.

They all stared at her in amazement. "You certainly know how to handle them," said Rikki, impressed.

"I should do. We've been together a good long

while." She paused and then her anger returned. "You've no right coming here, invading my home and making accusations about Miss Dinah. I've known her since she was a child – and her mother and father."

"You don't think she's capable of thieving?"

"Of course I don't. She's a tough lady – anyone who races ocean yachts with a male crew has to be. But that's all she is. Tough. She's always been so good to me and helped my research by letting me stay on this island. How dare you trespass on my property!"

Tim could see that she was getting very worked up. What was more, there was an edge to her that worried him, as if she were only just in control. What was she frightened of? Was it them or was there something else?

"What's your name?" asked Flower, in a very calm voice.

"Sarah James."

"My name's Flower, and this is my brother Brian and my cousin Tim. We're all members of Green Watch, an English conservation group. How long have you lived on the island?"

"Ever since I was nineteen." Sarah James looked at Flower with uneasy interest. "I'm happy here, studying the birds," she added defensively.

'We really have got a reason to be here," said Flower.

"Then I'd like to hear more!" she rapped.

"Do you ever leave the island?" asked Flower very quietly.

"Occasionally, to lecture, but as rarely as possible."
She seemed calmer now she was talking to Flower.
"Are you interested in birds?"

"Yes," said Flower swiftly. "If we get a chance,
can you tell me about them?"

"Well, we'll have to see what happens," she said
more sharply, and then softened again. "I like to
share what I know – what I can see – and you seem
like someone I could share with. I'd be interested to
hear about your group, too," she added with sudden
enthusiasm.

"Talking about sharing," Rikki interrupted, "I
would have expected Spark to be here by now. The
dogs have been making all this racket and he can't be
that far away."

Sarah James shrugged, "I'm sure I don't know
where he is, but maybe you'd better come upstairs
and sit down while we talk this over and decide what
to do."

"OK," said Rikki. "That seems a good idea."

Sarah James paused at the bottom of the ladder.
"Mr —?" she said, staring at Rikki doubtfully.

"Moon Shadow," he replied abruptly, looking
down at the wilderness below for signs of pursuit.

"You'd better come up."

Rikki winked at Green Watch, pushed past them
and began to climb the next flight of stairs. Lone
Wolf followed and then Tim, Brian and Flower.

As he climbed Tim kept looking back over his
shoulder. Where were Spark and his girlfriend?
Surely the barking and howling of the dogs would
have alerted them?

111

Green Watch were still climbing when a door swung open above them. As they breasted the second platform Tim saw Rikki and Lone Wolf disappear inside. Immediately there came the sound of a frantic struggle.

"What's going on?" yelled Tim.

"Wait!" Brian hovered indecisively. "Just wait!"

"Come on," shouted Flower, giving contrary instructions. "We've got to get in there."

Tim hauled himself up on the platform and followed her and Brian, who had suddenly changed his mind, into the dim interior of the second floor accommodation of the tree house.

The scene inside was one of formidable confusion. Rikki and Lone Wolf were lying on the floor while someone Tim could not immediately recognise was bending over them. Then he turned round and Tim gasped. It was Ray Spark.

"Tim again, isn't it?" he said. "How's it going?"

Tim stood staring up at him, unable to speak as his brain slowly and painfully told him that Sarah James had sprung a trap on them all.

"I'm very sorry," she said, speaking to no one in particular. "They were going to destroy my home and I couldn't bear that. It's part of me – all of me."

"Shut your mouth!" said a new, hard voice and Tim turned to see someone standing at the back of the room. She was very beautiful in a hard, glossy way, with long blonde hair and a tanned oval face. But her eyes were like chips of ice and Tim could feel a burning ruthlessness in her. The afternoon light was fading into evening now and the shadowed room was suddenly chilly.

"Come on, Ray, get it over with. We haven't got much time left." Her voice was as flinty as her eyes, Tim thought.

Tim looked down at Rikki and Lone Wolf. Both had blood on their faces and there was a gun in Ray Spark's hand.

Flower knelt down by Rikki and cradled his head in her hands. He muttered and tried to move but she pushed him back. An enormous bruise was coming up on his forehead. Spark must have hit them both with something, Tim thought. Maybe it had been the butt of the pistol.

"Leave him alone," rapped Dinah.

Flower gave her a look of withering contempt.

"And don't look at me that way either, you little —"

"I'll look at you any way I like," she rapped back.

"You want a slapping?"

"Try me."

Dinah suddenly burst out laughing and Ray Spark said, "Don't let her get to you; she's only a kid."

"A kid who'll learn a lesson," said Dinah, but Flower held her ground.

"Knock it off. We need to fix these two guys first." Spark levelled his gun at Rikki and Lone Wolf.

"What do you mean?" said Tim, finding his voice at last. "What do you mean, 'fix'?"

"Kill them," said Spark in an attempted matter-of-fact voice, but Tim could see that he was uneasy.

"Go ahead and do it," said Dinah. "And quick. We can bury their bodies on the island and they won't be found in centuries."

"It means doing for the kids too," said Spark.

Tim almost laughed aloud for he knew that he didn't mean what he said. It was as if he and Dinah were playing a game. Then he began to worry; Spark might not mean what he said but what about Dinah? She seemed much more ruthless.

"Why not?" Dinah challenged him.

"You won't be doing that." Sarah James's voice trembled but there was a determination to it as well. "You'll have to kill me first."

"Fine," Dinah scoffed. "I can always find another caretaker – not that I really need one."

"What about the dogs?" Sarah's voice was outraged.

"They're old. Time for them to be put down."

"You can't mean that."

"I mean everything I say. The island can rot while Ray and I take off to Europe. I've *had* America – I can race yachts anywhere."

"I don't believe —" began Sarah.

"Go on, Ray – kill them," Dinah shrieked. "Now." Spark hesitated.

"Or do you want me to do it?"

"You're a fake," said Flower to Dinah. "Just a big hulking fake."

"Keep out of it, you boring little girl."

"I may be boring but at least *I* don't have to dye my hair," said Flower sweetly.

Spark laughed involuntarily.

"Or is it really a wig, with a bald head underneath?" she went on.

"Why don't you girls knock it off?" said Ray Spark, looking amused.

"Keep quiet, Ray. I'm going to get this little slob."

"Baldie!" shouted Flower.

Tim glanced at Brian and wondered what he was thinking. He never gave much away. Flower was making a brave attempt, winding Dinah up like this, but he couldn't really see where it would get them.

"Flower, this isn't a game. These guys mean business." Rikki's voice cut through his thoughts.

Flower ignored him. She turned to Tim and said, "Isn't she ugly?" And then to Brian, "Let's get her wig off."

Guessing what she had in mind, Tim gazed at the gun. Spark had relaxed and his grip on it had slackened.

Meanwhile Dinah Rush had moved to within a few centimetres of Flower, her fists clenched.

"Don't touch my sister!" bellowed Brian.

"I can look after myself," Flower rapped back.

"Flower —" began Rikki again.

"OK," said Ray Spark with a grin. "Let's see the cats fight."

But there was to be no fight at all, for Sarah James intervened. Picking up a large wooden bowl from a side table she hit Dinah Rush on the head and she went down with scream of rage and pain.

Rikki took immediate advantage of Spark's distraction and knocked the gun out of his hand. It went off harmlessly in a corner, but the noise was incredibly loud in the confined space and there was an intense stink of cordite.

"Sit on her!" screamed Flower, as she leapt on the dazed but still cursing Dinah. Sarah James followed and together they pinned her to the floor while Rikki and Ray Spark both dived for the gun at the same time.

"Get off me!" spat Dinah Rush.

"Want more of the fruit bowl, do you?" yelled Sarah James. "I never was a violent woman but I'll pay you back for mistreating those dogs – so help me I will."

Dinah stopped struggling abruptly as the gun went off again and Rikki fell back, clasping his shoulder and crying out in pain. Suddenly the situation became deadly serious again.

"Get him!" yelled Tim, and he and Brian charged, but Lone Wolf was there before them as he dived for Spark's legs. Crashing to the ground, Spark smashed his head hard on the wooden floor and Lone Wolf twisted the gun out of his hand.

Flower rushed over to Rikki. "Where are you hit?"

"Arm. It's OK. Just a graze."

"Let me see."

"No, it's nothing." He pushed her aside and yelled

at Lone Wolf, "Cover him – but don't shoot him!"

"Not yet."

"What do you mean?"

Lone Wolf grinned. "I won't kill him yet – that's what I mean." He dug the barrel into Spark's head. "Where are the stones?"

"I'm not telling you."

"Where are they?"

"No way."

"So help me, I'll kill you. Tell me where the stones are."

Spark remained silent, although Tim could see his eyes were bulging with fear.

"Tell me *now*." Lone Wolf stared down at Ray Spark and there must have been something in his face that convinced Spark he really meant what he said.

"Look —"

"Tell me. Now!"

"OK."

"Where?"

"They're in the speedboat," he began.

"Shut up, you fool!" yelled Dinah. "Just shut up. He won't touch you."

"He knows I will," said Lone Wolf quietly.

"I said they're in the speedboat, down at the dock. In a box at the back, waiting to be handed over. Now take that gun away."

"You telling me the truth?"

"Yeah."

"I really believe you are. But I'm going to kill you anyway." Lone Wolf's voice was emotionless and Tim somehow knew that he meant exactly what he said. There was an intense hatred in his eyes as he whispered, "You tempted me, Ray, and I bought it, didn't I? I bought every bit of it. So this is from the Daiku —"

"Stop it!" yelled Rikki. "Now!"

"I'm going to kill you, Spark. You made me shoot the condor," whispered Lone Wolf.

"No." Spark's eyes were full of terror.

"It's your kind that pollute the world, Spark. Your kind that destroy the Daiku – destroy the condor. You're a parasite." Lone Wolf leant over and pressed the muzzle harder into Spark's temple while his finger tightened on the trigger.

Tim stared at them in horror. In his mind's eye he saw himself falling into the gully, rolling over and over towards the edge. Spark had saved him then; he must save Spark now.

Tim hurled himself at Lone Wolf and, taken by surprise, the Indian fell to one side, dropping the gun which Brian quickly grabbed. He threw it to Rikki who caught it and levelled the weapon at Tim, Lone Wolf and Spark, who were struggling desperately on the floor.

"Get up," he said.

Still they fought, panting, wrestling and kicking.

"Get up!" repeated Rikki. "If you don't stop, I'll shoot you in the leg, Lone Wolf. I want to save Spark and his lady friend for the police, and I'm going to make sure that happens."

Slowly, Lone Wolf separated himself from Ray Spark. "You're lucky," he sneered.

"I reckon we're quits now, Tim," said Spark, gasping for breath.

"You sentimental idiot," rasped Dinah Rush.

Chapter Eleven

"Where are the dogs now?" asked Rikki.

"They'll be in the woods," said Sarah James. "But they won't attack you if I'm with you. What are you going to do?"

"Leave the island," he replied, "like really fast. Once we get the stones."

"I'll find the dogs' food," she said. "They'll starve if I don't." She turned on Dinah and Ray in withering contempt. "How could you do that to them? Someone should do the same to you."

"OK," said Rikki to Ray Spark and Dinah Rush. "Both of you – back to back on the bed. Lone Wolf, find something to tie them up with."

"I've got something," pronounced Sarah James with grim relish. "Nothing would give me greater pleasure." She pulled out some nylon rope from under the bed. "I normally use this as a clothesline. It'll be ideal."

Dinah Rush and Ray Spark sat sullenly on the bed while Sarah lashed them together and tied them to the bedpost. Dinah watched her with fury, but all the fight seemed to have gone out of Spark.

"I'll be calling the police," said Rikki, and Tim watched a sneer curl Dinah's lips.

"You'll be lucky to do that. There's no phone on the island," she said.

"Yeah?" Rikki wasn't so sure. "Then how do you contact Chief Mono?"

"The arrangement was already made," she laughed. "Feel free to search if you want – you'll be wasting your time."

Rikki looked at his watch. "When do you expect him?"

"That," she said quietly and with some pleasure, "would be really telling, wouldn't it? Maybe he's here already, and of course he'll be armed."

But Flower wasn't listening. "It was she who led you into this," she said to Spark. "Wasn't it?"

Spark said nothing and Flower turned to Dinah furiously.

"You've got so much, haven't you? You still have money, a life of your own, freedom. The Daiku had nothing to build on but a bird that doesn't have a mate and a shrine that's lost its glory, thanks to you."

"A scraggy old bird and —" Dinah replied.

"And a fortune in precious stones," finished Flower. "They were sacred to them."

"Good luck charms," she snapped.

"Much, much more than that. But you went out of your way to get that fortune, didn't you? Using Lone Wolf. Using Ray Spark."

"Get lost!"

"It's true what I'm saying, isn't it?" said Flower. "And in the end you got nothing. Nothing but a weak man and a long prison sentence."

"Listen, you patronising little loser, I may be temporarily stuck with a weak man but I'm not going to serve any sentence. You know why?"

"Tell us," said Flower. "We don't mind listening to your fantasies. Not for a short time, anyway."

Dinah grinned infuriatingly.

"Listen, little girl, by the time you get to a phone we'll be gone. Chief Mono will have seen to that. And as for the stones, if you manage to get away with them this time, I'll give you a promise." She paused and then spoke slowly and more quietly. "I'll get them back however long it takes me, and I'll get you – if I have to come to the UK to do it. Do you understand, you pathetic little scrap of nothing?"

"Yes," said Flower. Her voice was steady but somehow Tim knew how afraid she really was. Suddenly he felt very sorry for her, and frightened for her too. Obviously Brian felt the same for he said to Rikki:

"Is there something we can put in that woman's mouth to stop the poison leaking out?"

"Yes," said Rikki. He turned to Sarah James. "Do you have something we could use as a gag?"

"You bet I have," she replied enthusiastically.

Even after being gagged with a large blue silk scarf, Dinah Rush's eyes still glowered at Flower. Rikki gagged Ray Spark too but he was clearly broken, and closed his eyes as if trying to blind himself to the fact that his dreams of a wealthy future with Dinah Rush were over.

"OK," said Rikki. "Let's get down to the harbour."

"One minute," said Sarah. "I *must* feed those dogs and then – when we've got this lot sorted out – I'll come back and look after them." She paused. "I suppose I *can* come back?" She stared into Dinah's eyes, which suddenly looked mocking. "Your mother would have wanted me to," she said fiercely, but then much of her bravado disappeared and Sarah turned to Rikki in alarm. "I *must* come back here. It's my home. I can't leave the birds. And then there're the dogs —" She broke off with a dry sob.

Rikki intervened quickly. "Fetch the food and let's go. You'll be back here – I guarantee that."

Sarah James reached out and touched his arm gently. She looks like a trusting little kid, thought Tim. But he knew that somehow Rikki wouldn't let her down.

Sarah James stood on the balcony of the tree house and banged a saucepan with a wooden spoon. The dogs were a daunting sight as they arrived in ones and twos, salivating, with huge mournful eyes. Sarah began to throw huge lumps of meat down to them and they rushed at it, tearing and snapping amongst themselves.

"I'll come back and fatten them up," she said.

"You must be careful," said Flower. "Won't they be dangerous?"

"No," she said confidently. "I shall know them and love them. I'll care for them, which is more than she ever did."

"Look," said Lone Wolf quietly. "The condor's here."

Suddenly she was high in the twilit sky, hovering over them.

"She hasn't gone back to Coyote," said Brian.

"Maybe she wants to see what's going to happen," replied Rikki quietly.

They walked unharmed through the alsatians and not one bothered to look up at them. Led by Sarah, they eventually came down to a small jetty where a speedboat lay rocking gently. The condor seemed to fly with them, losing height a little as they paused, and Tim had a feeling of companionship – of shared endeavour. It was very strange but the sensation calmed him, making the bizarre nightmare of recent events less traumatic.

"The box should be in the stern," said Rikki, and Tim ran ahead. Like everyone else, he was completely exhausted now and all he wanted to do was to get back to the mainland with the Daiku's heritage and sleep. Once on the jetty, he leapt into the boat and began to search, confident that their problems were over. The interior of the cockpit was simple, with no nooks and crannies, and so it was with a plummeting feeling in his stomach that he stared around the tiny space in mounting disbelief. There was no sign of any box.

"Stay where you are," whispered a soft voice and the feeling of terror gripped Tim's chest so tightly that he could hardly breathe.

Chief Mono emerged from the shadows of the boathouse with a hunting rifle in his hand. "Don't move, any of you." Someone else joined him – the bulky figure of a man in a business suit and an expensive-looking coat. Chief Mono grinned. "Leonard, I'm sure we'll find our colleagues somewhere on the island, but first of all I think we should dispose of some unwanted passengers." He smiled maliciously at Rikki. "I'm sorry. It's been a long time – all those years with the Daiku. I did believe once," he said. "I really believed, but I'm afraid that belief waned."

"To be replaced by greed," snapped Rikki.

"I've had nothing for too long."

"You were elected our chief," Rikki accused him.

"Yes, and it was that responsibility that made me realise the Daiku had no future."

"And you had?" muttered Brian.

"Something like that."

"What's up there?" asked Leonard, staring up at the night sky.

"Looks like a big bird."

"It's the condor," said Chief Mono, raising his rifle slowly and relentlessly. "She's got no future, just like the Daiku, so we might as well call a halt to it all now. Don't let's prolong the slow death."

"No," yelled Tim. "You *can't* kill her."

"It's better not to have false expectations," he replied quietly.

"Wait." Sarah James was walking towards him. "You'll not do that – you'll not kill that beautiful bird."

"Stay where you are."

"You'll not kill her." She continued to move purposefully towards him, and Tim saw that there was the same strength of determination in her eyes as there had been in Dinah Rush's. Human beings at the extreme of their endurance could show the most amazing power, he realised. But he was desperately afraid for Sarah James as she marched on Chief Mono like a conquering army.

"Put the gun down," she said.

Still the condor wheeled overhead, coming down even lower.

"Put it down!"

Chief Mono shook his head.

"Put it down." Her voice was soft and she was within centimetres of him now.

"Sarah, stay where you are. He's dangerous," said Rikki.

"I know," she said, reaching out for the rifle.

"Don't be a fool!" Lone Wolf gabbled. "Back off."

"Sound advice," grunted Chief Mono. The condor seemed almost stationary, presenting an ideal target. Leonard looked on, as if horrified by the confrontation, drawing his coat around him protectively.

"Put it down!"

"Go away." He aimed as he spoke.

"Give me the rifle." Her hand was outstretched.

"Back off, lady."

Still the condor circled. Let her fly away, prayed Tim. Please make her fly away.

Chief Mono's finger tensed on the trigger as the condor continued to hover, and Tim looked up at the strange, mystic bird, waiting for the shot to ring out and a bundle of bloodied feathers fall to earth.

She leapt at Mono just as he was about to fire, and for a moment they staggered, clasped together on the edge of the jetty. The rifle went off only once and Sarah James staggered back, blood staining her dress.

Before Chief Mono could do anything, Rikki and Lone Wolf had wrested the gun away and knocked him to the ground, while all three members of Green Watch rushed at the portly Leonard, not caring whether he was armed or not. But he didn't stand his ground and backed away until he fell off the jetty and plunged into the water with a resounding splash.

As Lone Wolf restrained Chief Mono, Rikki took his rifle and walked to the edge of the jetty, pointing it at Leonard who was staggering out of the water, his hands automatically raised in hasty surrender. But Tim wasn't watching; with Flower and Brian, he was bending over Sarah James who was lying on her back, blood spreading down her side. As Flower stroked her hair, Sarah looked up at the condor which was now flying a few metres above their heads.

"Beautiful," she whispered. "Just beautiful."

Then the condor soared and began to climb higher and higher. After a while she was lost to sight.

Epilogue

Tim only had the haziest recollection of their return journey. Rikki had disabled Ray Spark's speedboat and put the Daiku's precious stones in the back of his own. Then they had bounced back over the waves to the mainland. He had bound Sarah James's wound so tightly that at least the blood had stopped flowing, but she was unconscious by the time they arrived at Coronado and Rikki's first call had been the ambulance, the second the police. Then, at least to Tim, events grew even hazier. He vaguely remembered being questioned by a roughly kind cop, then staggering in at the door of the cabin on the beach and dragging out a bed. But none of them could sleep until they had found out how Sarah James was progressing, and eventually the hospital called back to say she was "comfortable and out of danger."

Tim fell into a deep sleep directly his head touched the pillow, and towards morning dreamt of Palm Canyon. He was searching the rocky clearings, desperately examining each and every stone until he found what he had been looking for. The condor's egg, large and blue and shiny, lay in a nest of straw underneath a palm tree. As Tim watched, the egg began to hatch and out of it poured dozens of the Daiku. The sky grew dark above them as the condor, now giant-sized, flew down. As she came nearer, the miniature Daiku raised bows and arrows and fired at her. Within seconds she had crashed to earth, suffocating the newly hatched fledglings. Then the condor's head became that of Sarah James and he heard the sound of distant barking.

Eventually Tim struggled awake to be told by Rikki that Sarah was definitely going to be all right, and that the police had arrested the four castaways on Serendipity Island.

That afternoon Rikki drove them back to Palm Canyon, to the Forest of Dreams where the Daiku had now gathered. In the background, leaning against a gravestone, was the dream-keeper and even further into the shadows Coyote, who had reluctantly agreed to leave his desert eyrie.

"Did the condor come back to you last night?" asked Tim.

Coyote nodded. "She was exhausted, but she returned. She's still sleeping in the shade of the rock."

It was late afternoon and the Forest of Dreams was shifting with mellow shadow. Rikki began to tell the assembled Daiku what had happened and to Tim it seemed that they were listening with a new energy, as if with the departure of Chief Mono they had been given new hope and could begin to wipe out the years of inertia.

When he had finished talking about the past, Rikki began to talk slowly of the future. "In a few minutes we'll light a fire round the shrine and put the precious stones back on the body of our sacred condor. And in doing this we shall make fresh start. The return of the stones is the start of fresh life to us. Old members of the tribe will return and this time we shall be strong enough to combat the taint of the city. I shall also redouble my work to fight for the return of our lands." He paused and as he did so Lone Wolf took his opportunity.

"We can only be strong if we have a strong leader," he said.

"Who then?" Rikki Moon Shadow looked around, genuinely wondering who Lone Wolf meant. But Tim knew and he was sure Flower and Brian did too.

"You, of course."

"But I can't —"

"You can," said Lone Wolf with great conviction. "And what is more, you must."

Rikki said nothing for a long while. Then he smiled at the Daiku and said, "It would be a great honour."

The tribe burst into spontaneous applause.

131

"There is something I must tell you," said Coyote, speaking for the first time. "Something some of us know already."

"Well?" asked Rikki hesitantly.

"Remember the naturalist I told you about who wants to find a mate for the condor? He's trying to get a project off the ground – a programme of re-introducing captive condors into the wild – and he wants to start by providing the mate for our condor next month." He paused. "It could be the beginning of a breeding colony here in Palm Canyon."

"That would be a miracle," said Lone Wolf.

"Yes," replied Coyote. "But they do happen – sometimes."

As they sat round the fire, watching the Daiku work to put the precious stones back into the body of the stone condor, Tim felt heady with elation and yet incredibly drowsy. Without thinking, he told the others that he wanted to dream.

"That's odd," said Flower. "That's what I want to do."

"Yes," said Brian. "So do I."

Tim looked up at the night sky. Was that the condor flying across the white face of the full moon, or was he already dreaming?